Novels by Martha Fouts

On The Mother's Day Tea . . .

"This story was sweet, charming, and reminiscent of all that I love about Hallmark channel. I really enjoy reading a story with a friendship turned romance! If you are looking for a sweet romance with relatable characters that draw you into their story, then you will really enjoy The Mother's Day Tea by Martha Fouts!
- *Ashley Johnson, Bringing Up Books reviewer and blogger*

On The Mother's Day Letter (audiobook version) . . .

"This is a beautiful story of learning to let go of control and trusting yourself and those around you. I adore Natalie. She is a strong, independent woman with a huge heart. The challenges she faces in this book are so relatable. Planning is how she deals with life, and when she gets a letter that throws that upside down, she pushes through and follows the advice she's been given. This book is written by a Christian author, and God plays a big part in this story. The narrator did an amazing job, and she even sings! This book made my heart happy!"
- *Chelsea Groff, book reviewer and blogger*

On Whispers & Dreams . . .

"Whispers & Dreams is one of the best stories I have read lately. Author Martha Fouts tells a story that kept me on the edge of my seat at times, had me crying at times, had me laughing at times and definitely made me want to keep reading and not put the book down. The story of

Melissa, Whisper, Dreamer and all the characters touched my heart. Several times while reading, I said out loud, "Oh my!" and "Oh, no, what's going to happen?" This is a great story."
- *Melissa Henderson, award winning inspirational author*

"Martha Fouts has given us a delightful story about finding yourself by listening to that still small voice in your spirit. The book kept me engaged until the end, and just when I thought it was over, Martha threw in a final twist that had me turning the pages even faster. Well done!"
- *Sharon Srock, author of women's Christian fiction novels*

On Christmas with Cameron Stinking Miller . . .

"A spirited and spiritual Christmas romcom! I loved everything about this sweet, clean, Christian romcom set during Christmas!"
- *Toni Cabell, award winning clean fantasy romance author*

"A heartwarming tale about the true peace that comes when you forgive others—and yourself. Yes, it's a sweet Christmas romance, perfect to get you in the mood for the holidays. But it also contains solid truth: our actions do matter, and they do affect others, but Christmas is a reminder that Christ came to provide lasting forgiveness and redemption. So that teenage boy who used to like to tug your pigtails may grow up to be just the one to remind you of Christ's perfect gift of love—even if it IS "Cameron Stinking Miller"
- *Elizabeth Daghfal, award winning short story author, blogger, and columnist*

"Hannah Orwell returns to her hometown for a job and runs into her childhood nemesis. We all have somebody from childhood who made our lives miserable, and that's one of the many ways this story is so realistic. It's touches the readers heart as Hannah must work with Cameron Miller. This story looks at themes of loving your neighbor and forgiveness. It's a love story, and once you read it, you won't forget it.
- *Jackie Layton, author of cozy mystery novels*

"Author Martha Fouts nailed it with this sweet romance, Christmas with Cameron Stinking Miller. Her characters will inch their way into your heart and you won't soon forget them. Her story is filled with love and laughter, real life hurts and forgiveness. And I dare you not to fall for

Cameron Stinking Miller—I did."
- *Jessica Ferguson, author of inspirational novels, novellas, short stories, poetry, inspirational non-fiction and drama*

"Christmas with Cameron Stinking Miller is a delightful story that manages to capture the development of a sweet romance while communicating deep truths about mistakes and forgiveness. I loved the main characters and was thoroughly caught up in their story. Highly recommend!"
- *Janet Joanou Weiner, missionary and author of Christian historical fiction novels*

"This was a sweet story of love and forgiveness. Reminiscent of a Hallmark movie, it is ideal cozy-up-with-tea reading. We all have that one person (or more!) in our past we would rather not see again. What would happen if our paths couldn't help but cross again?"
- *Emily Enger, writer, book marketer, and publicity coach*

Dedication

For my girls,
McKayla, Hannah, Jeslyn

The Mother's Day Bargain

Martha Fouts

"There's a part of all of us that longs to know that even what's weakest about us is still redeemable and can ultimately count for something good."
Fred Rogers

Chapter One

Rae's work phone buzzed, vibrating the rest of the items atop her pristine desk. She looked at the display. Carol Reed from the third floor. Again.

She pinched the bridge of her nose for a moment and then answered the call.

"Yes, Carol. How can I help you? Printer giving you trouble again?"

On the other end of the line, the older woman's voice sounded frantic. "Yes, it's not talking to my computer for some reason, and I need these reports to hand out at the lunch meeting that is supposed to start in five minutes."

Rae resisted the urge to groan. Why was this woman still printing reports? Seriously, Rae had been calling for all the printers in the building to be removed for this very reason. Paper was completely unnecessary.

"Carol, I would be happy to help you fix your printer, or you could also send the report to everyone in your meeting as an attachment to an email. Would you like to do that?" Rae hoped she sounded kind and not condescending.

"I know everyone wants me to do away with my paper reports, but I can't seem to do it. It feels like I'm cheating somehow. Can you just help me fix my printer?"

Rae felt sorry for Carol. She'd been with Garner and Fox Engineering for decades. The company had probably gone through many changes and operated much differently than when she first started.

"Okay, so, let's check your connectivity first. Do you remember how to do that?" Rae asked sweetly.

"Yes, I actually remember that from last time. I should have checked that before I called you."

"That's okay, Carol. That's what I'm here for. Does the wi-fi appear to be enabled?"

As Rae was talking, her friend Melody came into her office and sat in one of the uncomfortable guest chairs across from Rae's desk. Melody pointed at her phone and mouthed, "It's almost noon."

Rae nodded.

"There's an exclamation point over the wi-fi symbol. That means it's not connected, right?"

"Yes, that's right. Now, let's get you connected and you'll be printing in no time." Rae talked Carol through the steps to reconnect her wi-fi, and the woman rejoiced when her report successfully, and unnecessarily, printed.

"Thank you, Rae, you're the best. I don't know what I'd do without you." Carol thanked her breathlessly, no doubt talking as she ran to her meeting.

"Not a problem. That's what they pay me for. Have a good meeting." Rae hung up the phone and rushed around the desk to Melody. "Is it up yet?"

"Not yet. I've already got his profile pulled up on my phone. It's 11:59, so you're right on time."

Rae stood next to Melody and stared at her phone with her, waiting for the time to change to 12:00 and for her best friend's latest YouTube video to drop.

"He's such a dork. He said last night that he's thinking about not doing YouTube anymore. He said it's getting stressful trying to think of new stuff all the time." Rae shook her head and smirked. "Like he would throw away over thirty thousand views every week. Did I tell you how much new business he's gotten from that one short that went viral?"

"Sshhh!" Melody hissed. "It's noon! Here it is!"

Rae's best friend, Gabriel, appeared on Melody's phone, with a popular song from the early 2000's playing in the background. He stood next to his realty sign in the front yard of a house, and started dancing. Then, the video switched to him with a group of people inside the house with all of them doing the same dance. Then, the video switched to him next to his realty sign in the front yard of another house dancing again, and the video switched again to the interior of the house with a group of people dancing with him.

The video ended, and Melody sighed. "And just like that,

he will get another thirty thousand views. That guy can make a video of himself drinking a bottle of water and the world will want to watch it."

Rae laughed. "Exactly. He's always been like that."

And I was always known as the girl who lived next door to the cutest boy in school, Rae mused.

As if sensing her friend's thought, Melody asked, "It must have been something growing up next door to Gabriel Matthews."

"Yeah, it was something all right." For years she hoped some of Gabriel's popularity glitter would rub off on her, but it never did.

"You know what," Melody announced as if she'd discovered how to create an unbreakable encryption algorithm, "I just realized that being Gabriel Matthew's next door neighbor was like a vaccine!"

Rae raised an eyebrow at her.

"Hear me out. You saw the cutest, most charismatic and popular guy every single day of your life. You two learned how to ride bicycles together and waited on the school bus together, all that stuff. Maybe because you were exposed to him so much it made you immune to his magnetism. Maybe that's why you are the only woman on the planet who can be around the guy and not fall in love with him?"

Rae faked a laugh. She was a master at faking laughs when other women talked about Gabriel like this, because years ago she had been hopelessly in love with Gabriel – until she'd wised up about their relationship being forever and always nothing more than a friendship.

Her thoughts were interrupted by her personal phone vibrating with a text. She circled around to her desk and checked it. It was Gabriel asking what she thought of his latest video.

"Let me guess. It's him asking what you thought of it." Melody stood and propped a hand on her hip, like a know-it-all, a smirk playing on her lips.

Rae shrugged. "What can I say? We're friends."

"The very best friends. I know." Her friend walked toward the door, her perfectly creased slacks swishing. "Two best friends who have absolutely no romantic feelings for each other. Sure, sure." She winked back at Rae as she left her office.

Rae shook her head at Melody. She was used to her dramatics. She picked up her personal phone to tell Gabriel what she thought of his video when her work buzzed. Duty called.

She spoke with a secretary on the fourth floor, talking her through the steps in rebooting her crashed computer. Then, as she was about to respond to Gabriel's text, one of the lead engineers called her and asked her to come to his office so they could discuss a possible security hack to their system. The unexpected meeting lasted thirty minutes and afterward Rae had a to-do list a mile long to investigate the potential hack and to shore up all of their security measures.

She returned to her office right on time for her afternoon meeting with the head of IT at their branch in Georgia. Her colleague was a thorough guy, albeit dry and boring, but thorough, so their meetings normally ran long, and by the time they were finished, she was in desperate need of an afternoon dose of caffeine and sugar, so she picked up her personal phone and took the stairs to the bottom floor where there was a coffee cart.

Several of her co-workers must have also needed a late afternoon pick-me-up, because the line was long. The wait time would finally give her a chance to respond to Gabriel's text.

When she looked at her phone, she saw that she'd actually missed four texts from him.

Gabriel
What did you think of it?
No response? Uh-oh. It was that bad?
Seriously Spencer? You're killing me.
I'm moving to Antarctica.

Rae chuckled. She didn't know what she had done to be surrounded by such dramatic friends. She placed her order for a vanilla latte and texted him back while she waited on her coffee.

Rae
Sorry for the delayed response. Of course it was great. I don't really understand the point of it, but I don't really understand the point of anything on social media, but you were great. Extremely charismatic. I'm sure you'll get tons of new listings and clients through it.

His response was immediate.

Gabriel
Whew! I feel better. I just needed you to tell me it was good.

Her coffee was ready. She grabbed the latte and sipped it as she headed back up to her office, taking the stairs to increase her step count for the day. The coffee warmed her and also gave her the jolt she needed to finish out the workday. She felt her phone in her pocket vibrate again with a text.

Gabriel
Remember my sister is expecting us tonight. Sorry. It starts at 7. Again, sorry.

She smiled at his unnecessary apologies. She'd known his sister, Brisa, for her entire life. He didn't have to apologize for her.

Rae
It's fine. I'll go and hear her out. Besides, your mom's brownies are worth listening to Brisa's pitch.

She had agreed to hear a presentation Brisa wanted to make about her latest money-making idea, yet another multi-level marketing adventure, but Gabriel's mom, Evelyn, had promised to make brownies, so that made everything better.

When she got back to her office, she checked her email and her phone buzzed numerous times throughout the afternoon with people desperate for her help. A surveyor in the field needed help connecting to the server; a project manager thought he'd lost all of his work when his computer crashed, and he offered her a million dollars when she found it for him; someone in human resources fell for a phishing scam email, so she had to investigate its source and deploy a new spam filter and then write and send an email to the entire company once again educating them on how to identify phishing scams and avoid clicking on links in emails.

By five-fifteen, she was tired of talking to people. She thought about her earlier conversation with Melody about

Gabriel's popularity when they were younger and realized that she was more popular now than she'd ever been. All day people had been begging to see her. She laughed inwardly at the idea that maybe she went into IT so that she would be popular.

There was always more work to be done, but it was time to call it a day. She and Melody walked downstairs together. Melody had already changed into a band t-shirt and jeans, telling Rae that she was so excited for a live band she was going to see that night with a group of friends. She invited Rae to go with her sometime, and Rae politely agreed, saying it sounded fun, but secretly she hoped her friend would never, ever ask her to go see a live band. She couldn't think of worse torture than having to listen to loud music in a smoky club.

Well, maybe listening to Brisa's MLM pitch might qualify as worse torture.

Chapter Two

The last house showing of the day resulted in a sale. Gabriel submitted the offer and told the potential buyers that he expected to hear something soon. He also represented the sellers and knew they were anxious to sell, but he didn't tell the buyers that. The sellers accepted the offer in minutes, and less than an hour later, both parties were sitting around the table in the brokerage signing the contract.

Gabriel would profit more from the sale of this single house than he made all last month. He left his office wanting to celebrate so he called Rae as he got into his Jeep. She answered after the first ring.

"Spencer! Guess what?"

"Umm . . ."

"I just si –"

"Hold on!" She cut him off. "I want to guess."

He started the Jeep and groaned at her.

"You just sighted a wildebeest? You just silently won the lottery? You just sidestepped a pothole. Oh my goodness, are you okay?"

"Are you finished?" He pulled out into traffic and smiled at her silliness.

"Almost. One more. You just silenced a horde of zombies!"

"You done?"

"Yes."

He could almost see her dimple and ornery grin.

"Tell me your news, Gabriel."

"I don't think you want to hear it."

"Please, tell me your news. I really want to hear your news."

"Okay, since you asked. I just signed the contract on the Wilson house."

Rae gasped. "The one on Winchester Avenue? With the hideous orange stained glass and enormous black light fixture with the chains on the front porch?"

Gabriel winced at the thought of the monstrous exterior of the home he sold. "Yeah, that's the one."

"Who would buy that ugly thing?"

"Let's not worry about that. Let's just celebrate the fact that I sold it, Spencer. Sheesh."

"Oh, okay, sorry. Congratulations!"

He could hear voices in the background of where she was. He recognized them as his family members' voices. Shoot. She beat him there.

"You're already at my mom's?"

"Yes," He could hear her tone change. "please get here." She asked in desperation. His sister had probably already started in on her pitch.

"You know, I might sit this one out." He teased.

"Gabriel Leonard Matthews, you'd better get your skinny rear over here."

He laughed at the way she invoked his middle name and flipped on his turn signal to turn onto the street where he'd grown up, where his mother still lived and where Rae's mother, Lois Spencer, still lived next door, and where Joe and Paige Donnelly still lived on the other side of Lois, even all these years after their friend Chet had vanished.

"I'm coming. Turning onto Redbud now. See you in a bit."

With a threat to do him bodily harm if he didn't get there soon, Rae hung up as he turned into the Summer Valley neighborhood. He drove down the familiar street to his childhood home that stood at the end of the cul-de-sac, and he could see himself at nine years old building ramps for his bicycle on the sidewalk with Rae and Chet. He chuckled at the memory.

When his mom's house came into view, a leaden feeling hit the center of his chest and weighed his heart down to his gut. Dad's old work truck wasn't there. His mom hadn't been able to part with the truck for the first few months after his dad's death, and she was finally able to let it go this week. She'd sold it for less than what it was worth to a cousin wanting to start a roadside assistance business like "Uncle Leo" had for so many years.

Now, seeing the driveway without the old truck occupying its usual space felt like another blow, another reminder that dad was gone.

When he pulled into the driveway behind his sister's car, he told himself the same thing he did every time he returned home: *Don't look over there.*

But, just like every other time, he found himself looking at the house two doors over. Chet Donnelly's house. He could still picture their three bicycles thrown in the front yard and the three of them climbing the giant tree that stood in front of the house. He could still see Chet waving at him as he got into an unfamiliar sports car. It had been the last time anyone had seen the seventeen-year-old.

He shook off the feeling and prepared to enter the house. Gabriel Matthews couldn't enter a social gathering looking down. It didn't matter if it was only family and Rae and her mom, who were like family. Gabriel Matthews always brought the party.

"What's up, family? Let's learn about pyramid schemes and eat some brownies, people!" He heralded like an announcer at a professional wrestling competition.

"It's not a pyramid scheme, Gab. Ri. El." His sister, Brisa, flipped her long, wavy brown hair over her shoulder as she punctuated his name. "Now, sit over there on the couch next to Rae and Camila and listen up. This is actually a good business opportunity." Then, she called out to her son, "Beckham, get your uncle a brownie and a drink."

Gabriel obeyed his eldest sister and sat next to Rae who was eating a brownie and talking to his other older sister, Camila.

"Hi honey bun. Give me some sugar." His mom came out of the kitchen and kissed his cheek and squeezed his shoulder. "That video was good today. Bella showed me on the YouTube. You'll get famous from that one for sure." She pointed at him and returned to the kitchen.

"The goal isn't really to get famous, mom." He called after her, but even if she heard, she wouldn't understand. He had explained to her and to the rest of his family numerous times that his YouTube channel was simply a way to advertise his business. He had no desire to be famous. The goal, as always, was to be rich.

Brisa took her place in the center of the room and cleared her throat, commanding everyone's attention.

"Did I miss anything?" He whispered to Rae.

"Not really. Brisa tried to start but Bella and Brinley were arguing so she had to break that up, and then Camila had to feed the baby, and she wanted to wait until she was back. I think Byron is asleep in the recliner and if Brisa catches him, there may be violence."

Gabriel looked at his brother-in-law across the room in dad's old recliner. Yep, he appeared to be asleep. Rae was right. If Brisa caught her husband sleeping during her presentation, he would be a dead man.

Gabriel looked around the room but didn't see his other brother-in-law.

"Where's Charlie?" He asked Rae. "How did he get out of this?"

Rae shrugged, so he leaned over and asked his sister, Camila on the other side of Rae.

"Hey, where's your husband?"

Camila shifted the sleeping baby in her arms to rest her little head on her shoulder.

"He got called in to work. Had to cover a shift for someone who was sick."

"Hmph," was Gabriel's reply. He would trade places with Charlie in a minute. He'd rather be working at the fire station with the possibility of fighting a real fire than sitting here in his mom's living room listening to his sister drone on about another one of her "business opportunities."

"Listen up, everybody." Brisa, ever the oldest bossy one, called them to attention. "I'd like to tell you all about Sticker Cutie." She clicked a button on her laptop that was open on the end table next to her. Her computer was connected to the living room television, and a slideshow appeared with STICKER CUTIE in giant, pink bubble letters across the screen.

"Sticker Cutie is a company that started five years ago and is now a globally recognized brand."

"Globally recognized? Have you ever heard of it?" He whispered to Rae.

She didn't respond but gave him a look that said he'd better be quiet if he didn't want the wrath of Brisa.

"Think about it, you have the opportunity to put any image you want on a sticker of any size! Stickers for your laptop, stickers to wrap around your entire car, or stickers for the wall – goodbye wallpaper!" Brisa clicked through the images on her screen showing all of the amazing possibilities of stickers.

"Uncle Gabriel, you should put one on your car advertising your real estate business," his eleven-year-old nephew Beckham told him as he brought him a plate with a brownie on it and a glass of milk.

"You know, Becks, that's actually not a bad idea."

The boy smiled at his uncle, proud of himself, and then sat on the arm of the couch next to him.

"You could do that, Gabriel. There are so many uses for these stickers. In fact, I ordered some wall sized stickers with purple flowers because Bella wants to re-do her bedroom. There are so many possibilities." Brisa clicked a button and the screen changed to an image of a woman surrounded by stacks of money. "But that's not the main reason I called you all here today. Sure, I would love for you to buy stickers from me, but the real profit in this business will come if you sign up to become a Sticker Cutie Partner. Then, you can start your business like I have selling these amazing stickers that almost sell themselves and signing up more Cutie Partners under you. We all make money together. It's quite an opportunity, and you can do it all from the comfort of your own home, on your schedule."

Gabriel gave Rae a look that said it all. Another one of Brisa's pyramid schemes. If they all just signed up, she would make money. He forced himself to not groan. He wondered how much she expected them all to pony up this time. Last time it was a steak knife company, and they had to pay three hundred and ninety-nine dollars (divided up into three EZ payments!) to purchase the starter pack.

He respected his sister's motivation to make a lot of money. In fact, he identified with it. They'd both inherited that from their dad. But he had his own plan to build up his bank account, and he wasn't expecting any help from his family. Their dad had taught them that they would have to work for it themselves. It annoyed him that Brisa expected all of them to help her get there.

Brisa passed around a product catalogue, and all the women in the room politely looked at the sticker options and asked questions about creating custom stickers.

He patted his nephew's knee. "So, Becks, did the coach switch you to first base?"

Beckham nodded and wiped brownie crumbs from the corner of his mouth before he spoke. "Yes sir, he said I did really good so he's moving me in and putting Jake in my old spot in the outfield. I feel kind of bad for Jake, though. He's really upset about it."

The kid had always been soft-hearted.

"Hey Becks, don't feel bad about replacing your friend. You didn't want him to lose his spot. You just want the team to do well, right?"

"Yeah, I guess so."

"Byron!" Brisa yelled at her husband when she noticed that he was asleep.

The big man jerked awake, nearly causing the recliner to tip over.

Beckham stifled a giggle at his parents, and Gabriel laughed for him.

After rebuking her husband, Brisa made her way to the couch where Camila, Rae, and Gabriel sat.

"What do you all think? It's a pretty good business plan, isn't it?"

Gabriel loved his sister, but he had decided after the steak knives that he was finished with her "businesses."

"I think I will buy one of those stickers for the Jeep. The price isn't bad at all. I'll order it from you tonight and send over the artwork tomorrow, if that works for you." He stood with his plate and glass in hand.

"Thank you, Gabriel. I appreciate that. What do you think about signing up for the business?"

Leave it to Brisa to not let it go.

"Brisa, I already have a business that keeps me busy. I really don't need another one. Thank you for offering, though." He patted her shoulder and headed for the kitchen before she could respond.

The family kitchen felt more like home than any other room in the house. According to the latest decorating trends, it was totally out of style, but to him, it was timeless. From the brick pavers on the floor and the pot rack that hung over the center island to the pale blue cabinets and the wooden ceiling cross beams overhead, this was the heart of his childhood home. This was where the family of five had all of their breakfasts and dinners, with a mom who was an exceptional cook and a dad who prayed before the meals and told jokes during them.

He took his plate and glass to the sink and washed them and set them in his mother's drying rack.

"Come sit next to me, my sweet boy." His mom called to him from the kitchen table where she sat across from Lois Spencer. The two of them had tea cups with strings hanging over the sides ending with little paper squares. Steam emanated from their dainty cups as the two old friends sipped their tea and chatted.

"How did you ladies get out of Brisa's presentation?" He asked them with a sparkle in his eye. He sat next to his mom, and she gave him a side hug.

"Oh, when you get to be a certain age, people quit pressuring you to do dumb stuff." His mom answered succinctly.

"I'm not saying Brisa's businesses are dumb," Lois, ever the diplomat, said with a raised hand as if swearing into a trial. "I think she just hasn't found the right business yet. That young lady is an entrepreneur. She's going to make a lot of money one day." She glanced over the tops of her glasses into the living room and added with a whisper, "Now, it's probably not going to be with this dumb business, but one day."

She and Gabriel's mom cackled at the joke, and it reminded him of all the times the two friends laughed like that in this very kitchen with those very same tea cups.

"All right, all right you two. You'd better quiet down, or they're going to come in here and make us join them. Do you ladies know what very important day is in less than two weeks?"

Evelyn took a sip of her tea and answered him as if she saw him coming a mile away. "Oh we know, Mr. Famous. We know. It's in eleven days."

Lois was also two steps ahead of him. "Your mother and I were just talking about that. We've got a plan."

Evelyn shook her head at Lois and said, "Not now, dear."

What was this? A plan?

"Oh, you two have a plan for Mother's Day?"

His mom took another sip and answered, "Yes, dear. Since

it's the first year without your father, I'd like to combine our celebration with the Spencers, if you and your sisters don't mind. Lois said she and Rae and Claire would love to join us for lunch after church that day."

That was the plan that his mom was acting so secretive about? He doubted it. These two were hiding something that they were cooking up in this kitchen.

"Sure, that sounds fine. You Spencers are like family." He reached across the table and patted Rae's mom's hand. He loved his mom's partner in crime like family.

"You must be excited that Claire is coming home. When will she be here?" He asked Lois about Rae's spunky younger sister.

"She's zooming in the morning of Mother's Day and zooming out that evening," Lois shook her head at her youngest child. "That girl won't even be here twenty-four hours, but you know Claire."

He did know Claire. He loved her like a sister, but he much preferred the calm and easy-going eldest Spencer daughter.

Brisa came into the kitchen in her regular whirlwind of energy and determination.

"Hey you three, can I talk any of you into signing up to be Cutie Partners? Camila signed up. I'm sure she would love another family member joining her at the Charming Level."

So, she had talked Camila into it. He wasn't surprised. Camila usually did whatever necessary to keep the peace and make everyone else happy.

"Brisa, you're one of my favorite sisters, but – "

"One of your favorite sisters?" She cut him off. "What do you mean? You only have two sisters."

"Exactly." He put both hands on her shoulders and looked her squarely in the eyes. He wanted to make certain she heard him "And if you don't stop trying to sign me up for your businesses, then you are going to fall out of that spot, and Camila will be my favorite."

Her mouth opened, but nothing came out, which was a rare occurrence for Brisa.

"We don't want that to happen, now do we?" He leaned forward and kissed his sister's forehead. "Love you, sis."

He turned back toward the living room where Rae still sat on the couch. "I just remembered we had that thing we were supposed to do tonight. We'd better go now. We're almost late as it is."

He was lying through his teeth. They had no "thing," but he could tell she was ready to ditch the Sticker Cutie party as well, so he hoped she would play along.

"That's right! We told Brooklyn we'd stop by her store tonight. She's unveiling a line of cookies at the bakery, and we said we would get some and post them on Gabriel's Instagram. You know, helping out a friend." She stood and put on an 'aw, shucks, sorry we have to leave' expression.

After disentangling themselves from everyone's objections to them leaving early, Rae and Gabriel stood on his mother's driveway and laughed.

"Now I have to go to Brooklyn's bakery and make an Instagram post, or we're going to be liars."

She grinned at him. "Too bad. We're going to have to get some of her cookies."

He laughed with her, and they decided to take his Jeep and leave her car parked at her mom's house where he would bring her back to get it.

They jumped into his Jeep and headed to Be Sweet Bakery to get some cookies. They talked non-stop – about everything. Nothing was off limits. They talked about neighbors whose houses they passed and their jobs and relatives. She talked about achieving her step count goal for the day, and he told her how someone that day had thought he was his broker's son and how mad that had made him. His broker, Greg, was fifteen years older than Gabriel, and hated that he was getting older. Gabriel told Rae that he thought Greg got Botox injections to cure his wrinkles, and Rae laughed.

They stopped at the bakery and chatted with their old friend and bought some cookies from her. Gabriel spent a few minutes making an Instagram reel bragging about the bakery and showing off Brooklyn's cookies. He uploaded it, and Brooklyn thanked him. Knowing how well he'd done with social media marketing, it was likely that the video would bring her quite a bit of business.

Rae and Gabriel said goodbye to Brooklyn and hopped back into the Jeep, each with a cookie in hand. As they drove through downtown Cool Springs, they both rolled their windows down and enjoyed the warm evening breeze.

"Spencer, I'll never understand why you waste your time on desserts that aren't chocolate. Why in the world would you choose a lime cookie?"

"Excuse me," she sighed defensively and held up the green cookie with white icing. "It's a key lime pie cookie, I'll have you know, and it is delicious. Not everything has to be chocolate, Gabriel."

He took a bite of his chocolate chip cookie and responded with a mouthful, "Of course it doesn't have to be, but why wouldn't you want it to be?"

Just then, the Jeep jerked and sputtered and died.

"What was that?"

He looked at his dashboard and then smacked his forehead. He'd let it run out of gas.

She leaned over and looked at the dash also.

"You ran out of gas?" Her eyes wide in shock. "Gabriel Matthews. You are thirty-four years old. How in the world can you run out of gas . . . again? Sheesh, Gabriel. You have got to start paying attention.

He shrugged. "I don't know. I see that it's running low and think about going to a gas station, but then I get preoccupied and forget." It was true. He had a very short attention span, and the next bright and shiny thing often stole his focus away from what needed to be done. He was able to force the engine to start for a second and then he coasted it into a parking space on the side of the street.

"Sorry about this Rae, but I've started carrying a gas can. We are only a couple of blocks from a station. I'll go get some gas really quick. You sit here, and I'll be right back." He started off toward the nearest gas station, but stopped when he heard her behind him.

"Hold on. I'm coming."

She got out of the Jeep and joined him. She was still wearing what she'd worn to work and looked out of place on the street in her blazer and slacks and loafers, but she jogged toward him anyway, ready for their next adventure. That was Rae. She was always up for an adventure, and he loved that about her.

"Spencer, we probably just added hundreds of steps to your day's total. You're welcome."

"Gee, thanks. I also had a brownie and a cookie tonight, so I'm not so sure how that all works out in the end."

"Ah, calories, schmalories. Skip breakfast tomorrow, and that will make up for it."

She shoved him with her shoulder. "Spoken like a true man. With all of your sisters you'd think you'd know that is not how it works for girls."

He was baffled. It wasn't? "But that's how it works for guys. Why isn't it the same?"

"It's one of the mysteries of life, my friend, one of the mysteries of life."

They walked in silence for a while down the familiar street of their hometown. The sidewalks were empty and almost every business was closed. Cool Springs wasn't exactly known for its swinging night life. He snuck a glance at her profile. She was looking up at the sky as they walked. She seemed to be completely content to be at his side walking down the street to a gas station.

And, in some ways, he felt the same. He was completely content with her by his side. But he also wasn't content, because he wanted something more with her, but he had no idea how to make that happen.

He closed his eyes for a brief few seconds and silently asked God if He could answer this one little prayer – if he and Rae Spencer could possibly be more than just friends.

Chapter Three

Thursdays were nose-to-the-grindstone days at Garner and Fox Engineering. The firm was only open until noon on Fridays, so most people tried to get as much work done as possible on Thursday so they could actually leave by noon the next day. That meant that Rae's phone rang constantly the entire day. People were in a rush, and if their tech wasn't working, then they got irritable. She had to make sure to put on her thick skin on Thursdays.

Gabriel
Wanna hang out tonight? I don't have any showings!

The text from Gabriel came while she was on her way up to the fifth floor to see her boss. She texted him back while she was taking the stairs two at a time.

Rae
Sure, let's go the Community Center. Pickleball?

Gabriel
Yes! See if Melody wants to come. I'll try to get Byron and Brisa or Charlie to come. We will dominate – as usual!

Rae laughed at his excessive exclamation points. They actually hadn't played in a while, since he'd been so busy with showings in the evenings, but back in the winter when they were playing almost every week, they were a great team. They usually played Brisa and Byron. Sometimes Charlie would come, but Camila had never been into sports, so Melody had come a few times and been his partner. Sometimes they played random people at the Community Center, but no matter who they played, Gabriel and Rae always won.

She looked at the time on her phone. Two o'clock. She just

had to grind for three more hours. She had no idea what her boss, the director of information technologies, needed her for, but he was usually an email guy, so when he had called her and asked her to come up, her interest was piqued.

The fifth and sixth floors were the top two floors and were the prettiest in the building. The first four floors were mainly cubicles and boring offices with uncomfortable furniture and potted plants with bland modern art on the walls, but the fifth and sixth floors were where all of the big wigs had their offices, so they were bright, gleaming spaces with wide windows and chrome fixtures and luxuriously covered furniture.

Mr. Ellis was her supervisor. (His first name was Dennis, but she would never, never call him by his first name.)

She rapped on the frame of his open door. "Hello, Mr. Ellis."

He was sitting behind his desk studying his computer. He looked up at her and smiled, his two large front teeth, sticking out over his bottom lip.

"Thank you for being so prompt, Rae." He waved to a plush blue velvet chair in front of his desk. "Please take a seat."

He found a file on the corner of his desk and handed it to her.

"An environmental engineer from our Georgia office will be working with our team on the Phillips project. Probably be here for a month or so. His name is Carter Stayton."

Rae opened the file and scanned the scope of his project and the list of tech he needed and information he would need access to. Mr. Ellis was probably asking her to set up a temporary office for this guy, something that wasn't at all uncommon for her to do. It usually took a few days to get everything up and going, so she assumed this Carter Stayton would be arriving on Monday.

"He'll be here tomorrow."

Surely, she had heard him wrong. "Tomorrow?"

"Yes," Mr. Ellis twitched his nose, as if he smelled something bad. "I know it's rather short notice, but I only just found out myself. It seems they've gotten themselves into some governmental trouble with this Phillips project, and Mr. Stayton is a real guru when it comes to environmental regulations, so the powers that be want him here and ready to work tomorrow. I'm sure you can get his office and tech up and running by tomorrow, can't you?"

"Yes, Mr. Ellis. I can certainly have that done by tomorrow."

"Thank you, Rae. That's why I asked you. I knew you could handle it." He reached across the desk and shook her hand.

Rae left his office and paused for a moment in the lobby. The fifth floor lobby. Many of the offices on this floor had their own bathrooms and the conference rooms were equipped with kitchenettes. The people who worked on this floor and on the one above it decided the direction of the company, set goals, cast vision, wrote policy, decided which projects they would take, had their names on the tops of letterhead, led meetings, and made multiple times more money than she made.

She decided to do something out of character and forgo the stairs and take the elevator. She pushed the lighted button and waited.

"Thank you, Rae. That's why I asked you. I knew you could handle it," her boss had said.

She'd heard people say things like that to her for her entire life.

"Let's ask Rae to be the stage manager. She doesn't like talking in front of people, anyway."

"My sister, Rae, is the world's best proof reader. I have her edit all of my stories before I send them anywhere."

"Rae, can you housesit for us while we go on family vacation? You don't have any plans of your own, after all."

Of course, she said yes to Mr. Ellis, because that's what she did. That's who she was. She'd always been in a supporting role, long before she ever had a career as tech support. Now that it was actually her job to make sure that everything ran smoothly for everyone else, she felt destined to stay in this same position.

The elevator doors opened for her, and she entered the empty elevator, taking another look at the sleek and sophisticated fifth floor before the doors slid closed. She couldn't imagine herself with an office on one of the top floors, even though she was one of the best IT specialists in the company and Mr. Ellis was probably less than five years from retirement.

She pressed the button for the second floor and thought

about the future of her career. She wished she could be one of those upwardly mobile people, like her friend Melody or like Gabriel. She wished she could take Mr. Ellis's job when he retired, and then maybe even keep moving up over the years. She was only thirty-four, after all.

But the warped reflection of herself in the shiny elevator doors reminded her who she was. Her mousy brown hair, sensible outfit, and flat shoes communicated loud and clear that she was the sidekick, the best friend, the supporting role. She had never been the star, and it was fine. She'd learned early on that she was at her best when she was behind-the-scenes helping, and that was just the way it was.

The elevator doors opened on her floor, but she decided that she needed a boost to get through the afternoon, so she pressed the button for the first floor where the coffee cart was calling her name once again.

After ordering her coffee, a thought struck her.

Is a supporting role all you ever want? Are you satisfied with being tech support in your career and nothing more than the faithful best friend to Gabriel? Thirty-four and not married and no boyfriend and no potential romantic interest anywhere in sight? No plan for career advancement?

While she waited on her coffee order, she continued with the line of thought.

Your birthday is next month. You'll be thirty-five. Thirty-five! Shouldn't people have some sort of potential life partner and career goal by the time they're thirty-five?

The coffee cart guy called her name and shook her out of her thoughts. She thanked him for the latte and took a sip and tried to take control of her thoughts.

It's fine. You have a steady, reliable job in a stable company, and several good friends. Wishing and hoping are for the movies and fairy tales. You need to live in reality, she scolded herself as she took the stairs to her office.

Back in her office, she closed the door and turned on praise and worship music at low volume to quiet her inner dialogue and opened the folder so she could get started on the temporary office for Carter Stayton. She arranged an office space for him on the third floor that she had outfitted for another temporary engineer several months ago and was still empty. She secured all of the hardware he'd need in the office and set up his network permissions. She was buzzing through her to-do list at a record pace when her personal phone rang. It was her mom.

She looked at the clock. She would take a break and give her mom a few minutes.

"Hey mom, how's your day?" Rae leaned back in her chair, the softly playing worship music and brief work break eased her tension.

"It's been lovely. Evelyn and I had our morning walk, and then I had to take Arlo to the vet for his ear mite surgery, and now he's resting, so I've been trying to be quiet, so I came outside to talk."

Rae stifled a giggle. Her mother treated her dog, Arlo, like he was a human. She was certain that since he had surgery today that her mom would treat him like a king for the rest of the week.

"Also, your sister texted and told me that she got that new job she wanted. She was so happy."

"The one at the big publisher? Oh wow, that's wonderful!" Rae meant it. Her younger sister was near completing her Masters of Fine Arts at Northwestern and had been hoping to be hired as an editorial assistant at Williams and Sons Publishing in London.

"I suppose it's wonderful."

Her mom sounded less than enthused, and Rae knew why.

"I'll miss her too, mom, but she's chasing her dreams, and she's taking care of herself. We should be proud of her."

"But London? It's so far away. I've never even been there. All I know about London is what I see on TV and in the movies – Big Ben, those snooty-looking black taxi cabs, people with royal titles and Buckingham Palace. How can I tell her what to watch out for? How can I give her any guidance at all?"

Rae's heart hurt for her mother. She knew her younger sister's unlimited ambition scared her. Shoot, it scared Rae too.

"Oh mom, you've always known what to say, because you let the Holy Spirit guide you. You don't have to live in a big city to have godly wisdom. Besides," Rae had to add, "you've raised a very self-sufficient young woman. Not many twenty-five year olds have achieved what Claire has. She's going to be just fine in London, mom."

"I know, dear. Thank you for reminding me. I've raised two incredible daughters. Even though they've taken completely different paths – one achieving grand things in London and one living a quiet life here in Cool Springs – I'm so proud of both of them."

Rae knew her mom meant her words as a compliment, but the stark juxtaposition of her sister's life and hers reminded her all over again that she would always be the boring older sister who made smart, careful choices and existed in the background of everyone else's lives.

"I had another reason for calling, dear. I want to present a challenge."

"A challenge, huh? What are you challenging me to, mom? A drag race? A duel?" Rae teased.

"Oh hush, you. I am issuing a Mother's Day challenge. You know how we're going to Evelyn's for lunch that day?"

"Mm-hmm," Rae intoned, wondering where her mother was going with this.

"Well, Evelyn and I decided to challenge you and Gabriel to bring a date to the lunch, and if you don't bring a date, then you'll allow us to set you up with someone!" She ended brightly, as if it was the best idea ever.

Rae snorted. "Mom, why would I agree to that?"

"Because it's Mother's Day, and it's the only thing I'm asking for," she quickly retorted. "I don't want any other present. This is all I want."

Her mother didn't usually play the guilt card, but when she did, she played it masterfully. She didn't verbalize that she'd raised Rae and Claire all on her own after their father died, but that went without saying.

Rae groaned. She couldn't say no to her mom.

"So, the deal is that if I can't find my own date that you have permission to bring a date for me?"

"That's right," her mom sounded smug. "Is it a deal?"

"Okay mom, you've got a deal, but don't start looking for my date. I can handle it. I'll bring a guy."

Now it was her mother's turn to snort. "Sure you will, honey, sure you will."

Chapter Four

Gabriel concluded the tour of the open concept office space with the husband and wife and told them that he would leave them alone for a few minutes so they could discuss the property freely. He told them that he would be right outside in his car if they needed him. The couple thanked him, and Gabriel got out of their hair. He could sense that they wanted to be alone.

His car was often his mobile office. He called, texted, and emailed potential buyers who had asked for his help in the search for the perfect house, office space, neighborhood lot, or commercial property, asking if anyone wanted to look at anything that afternoon. He got a couple of yeses and scheduled tours. Then, he scrolled through social media for research. Facebook, Instagram, and especially his YouTube channel had been an unexpected boon. Who knew that corny videos would so effectively increase his business?

The truth was, he felt like an idiot doing the videos. He was a grown man. It was embarrassing to do dances and lip-sync videos. He'd started out showing homes and giving real estate tips, like how to stage your home for a showing, or everything you need to know as a first-time home buyer, but somewhere along the way he'd branched out into the silly videos, and that was when he really got attention.

And the attention from the goofy videos had driven people to his real estate videos, which had increased his client base, so it was a good thing, but he couldn't help feeling dumb for being a thirty-five-year-old man who made dancing videos of himself. When his dad was thirty-five, he was married, already had three kids, and ran a successful roadside assistance business. There was no way on this planet that Leo Matthews would've ever made a video of himself dancing.

But, if it made him money, then it was worth it. He would lip sync, dance, do dumb tricks, whatever he needed to do to make money and build his business. He'd built both a successful real estate business and rental property management company from the ground up in his hometown, and his bank account was growing, and that's all that mattered.

The Garcias exited the office space and waved to him. He opened his car door and stepped out and gave them a grin.

"What's the verdict? Will it work for your dream business?"

The couple had told him that they wanted to open a co-working office space that could double as an event center that could be rented out for gatherings on the evenings and weekends – a unique concept that little Cool Springs didn't have yet.

"We do!" The wife answered. "But do you think they'll take less than their asking price?"

Gabriel shrugged. "It can't hurt to ask!"

It was a beautiful day, so they sat on a bench on the sidewalk in front of the property and decided on their official offer. Gabriel told them that he would submit it to the seller immediately and tell them as soon as he heard something. They thanked him and shook his hand and said good-bye, and then Gabriel was off to another showing.

He buzzed around Cool Springs and the surrounding communities all afternoon. He didn't fix cars like his dad did, but he had the same restless itch. His dad was always on the move, responding to calls for help, people broken down on the side of the road or in a parking lot. Just like his dad, he couldn't imagine working in one spot all day.

At a stoplight, he rolled down his window and rested an elbow on the door. He looked through his sunglasses at the wide blue sky and thanked God for the opportunity to work like this. He would go bonkers if he had to work inside all day, behind a desk staring at the same walls day after day.

"Hey Gabriel!" Someone called to him from the sidewalk with a wave.

He didn't know who they were, but he waved back like a homecoming king on a parade float.

He met three other clients for showings and was on his way to his fourth and final appointment when he realized that he was probably going to be late for pickleball. He opened his mouth to tell his phone through his car Bluetooth to call Rae, but the robotic voice of his phone spoke before he did.

"Incoming call from Mom." The robot voice told him while he flicked on his turn signal to turn into the neighborhood of the house he was showing. Ugh, mom. He loved her, but phone calls with her were usually marathon length.

"Hey mom, I'm actually about to get out of the car for a showing. Did you need something, or can I call you back later?"

"Humph, that's a fine greeting for the woman who gave birth to you. You do know that I carried you ten days past your due date, and that you weighed nine pounds and seven ounces, and that I didn't take any drugs, because I didn't want my baby to be born on drugs. Can you imagine giving birth to a nine pound, seven ounce baby? I'm sure you can't, but fine, Mr. Busy. You just call me back later."

Gabriel turned into the driveway and ran a hand over his face. Guilt was his mom's native language.

"I'm sorry, mom. I shouldn't have answered the phone that way. I love you, mom. How are you today?"

The lookers hadn't arrived yet, so he would talk to his mom before they arrived.

"I love you too, dear, and my day has been average. Someone knocked on the door and offered to inspect our roof for hail damage, because they said we might need a new roof, and I really didn't know what to say, because your dad always handled things like that."

"Did you let them inspect the roof?" There had been a hail storm a couple of weeks ago, so her roof may have had damage, but he hoped she didn't sign a contract with some random door-to-door salesperson.

"Yes, and they said we had some damage, and that I needed to report it to my home owner's insurance and that they could manipulate the numbers so that I could actually make money on the deal."

"Oh no, mom, you didn't."

"Now, I know I'm an old widow, and I've never handled things like this, but I'm not stupid, dear. Of course, I didn't agree to anything with them."

He let out a breath. Thank goodness.

"I told them that my son would talk to them, so I'll send you their number and you can call them, okay?"

"Yes, send me their number, and I'll talk to them." He wanted to be the one to help his mom. His dad would have wanted him to step up and take care of her, as the only son, but it made him miss his dad all over again. He'd been gone for nine months, and calls like this brought a fresh ache to his heart. He wondered when, if ever, that aching would go away and it would feel normal that dad was gone.

"Thank you for doing that, dear, and I have one more thing to talk about. Do you need to go do your showing, though? I can call you back, if I need to."

"No," he craned his neck to see up and down the street, "no sign of them, and they're ten minutes late. I may have been stood up."

"Okay, good."

"Good that I got stood up? Thanks, mom."

"Oh hush, you know what I mean." She paused. "Just a minute honey. Paige Donnelly is taking her dog for a walk in front of the house. I want to say hello."

He waited while he listened to her attempt conversation with her former friend. He could hear his mother's kind greeting and polite comments, but he couldn't hear Mrs. Donnelly's responses. A few moments later, his mom was back.

"Did she respond this time?" He asked. Paige Donnelly had practically become a recluse since her son's disappearance nineteen years ago. She and his mom and Rae's mom had been close friends, just like their children were, but all of that changed after the tragedy.

She took a deep breath, and Gabriel imagined her settling into her padded chair on the patio with a cup of tea while holding the phone between her cheek and shoulder, like he'd seen her do a million times.

"She said, "Hello," but that was all. My heart breaks for that poor woman. Her life has been shaped by tragedy."

They were both quiet for a moment. Chet's disappearance had been a tragedy for all of them. Gabriel found himself still thinking of his old friend and wondering where he could be, but the tragedy had profoundly changed Paige Donnelly. The once pleasant and talkative neighbor now spent her days in her house with no visitors, rarely venturing out into the world that had stolen her son.

"Son, you always give me a good Mother's Day present, but I've decided what I really want. I don't want you to go out and buy me anything this year, but I do want something big."

Her speech sounded prepared. He smiled at her. This was clearly important to her.

"Something big, but you don't want me to buy anything? I'm intrigued." He teased her.

"Yes dear, I'd like for you to please bring a date to the lunch."

As she took a breath and paused, he started to object, but kept quiet instead. He hadn't dated since his dad's death and had no interest in starting back up, but this was his precious mom who'd been through a lot lately, so he would hear her out.

"And I know that you haven't dated in a while and that you're very busy with work, and that there probably aren't a lot of women in Cool Springs you'd be interested in dating, so if you can't find anyone to bring to the lunch, then I'll bring a date for you."

He laughed out loud at that. "Oh you will, will you? And where will you find this date?"

"Leave that to me. In fact, I want my Mother's Day present to be a deal . . . or a bargain. If you can't find a date, then you agree that I can find one for you." She finished triumphantly, and he imagined her sitting back in her patio chair with a flourish.

"That's all you want for Mother's Day? Just me to have a date to the lunch, and if I can't find one, then you have to provide one?" It could be worse. At least he had a chance to pick his own date, and she wasn't forcing a blind date on him. "Okay, mom, if that's what you want."

"Hooray! I have to call Lois. I'll let you go and do your showing now, dear. Talk to you later."

She hung up before he had a chance to say goodbye, and he laughed at her again. Now the people he was supposed to meet were fifteen minutes late, so he figured they were a no show. Good. He wouldn't be late for pickleball after all.

The Cool Springs Community Center had been the result of a grant from Murphy Oil, the biggest employer in town. The center was only five years old, but it had already become a staple in the community. Gabriel went there at least three times a week to work out or play racquetball or basketball or pickleball. He wished the town would've had something like this when he was a teenager. He probably would've gotten into a lot less trouble.

Well, actually, he reconsidered that as he drove to meet Rae and the others. Would he have gotten into less trouble? Everything had come so easy to him back then – girls, friends, popularity, sports, grades – that he had been a supreme, colossal jerk. He thought the world orbited around him and that people had been created for his enjoyment.

He shook his head to make himself stop thinking about the past. That was how he had been "BC" or "before Christ," as Pastor Kevin put it. He'd changed his ways after becoming a Christian in college, and his pastor had reminded him a few times that he was a new creation and he no longer needed to feel condemned for how he had acted in the past.

Gabriel pulled into the Community Center parking lot and whispered a prayer of repentance for how he'd acted all those years ago, even though he had repented of the same thing many times over. As he unbuckled his seatbelt, he caught a glimpse of Rae entering the front door of the center with Byron and Brisa. She was laughing at something.

Gabriel smiled. That was his favorite laugh of hers. She had several types of laughs, but that one was his favorite. It was the one that made her throw her head back and caused tears to come out of her eyes.

Of all the people that he'd treated badly, he had treated Rae the worst. He was fully aware that he didn't deserve her friendship now. In high school he had known that she had a crush on him, and he'd used that to manipulate her. He got her to write essays for him; he'd hang out with her when he didn't have other options. He would even flirt with her just to see how she would light up from it, simply because it boosted his ego. When he ran for class president (and won), it had been Rae who made all of his posters and even wrote his speech.

He'd also known that Chet had a crush on Rae, and it made Gabriel feel powerful that she liked him instead. He'd been horrible to both of them. His two best friends.

He whispered a prayer asking God to help him be a better

person. He knew he had been forgiven, but he also knew that change was required. He wanted to grow in Christ to become the person God wanted him to be. He pulled his gym bag over a shoulder and got out of his car and headed inside.

He was determined to be a good friend to Rae now. He couldn't make things right with Chet, but he could make things right with her. She'd been nothing but a friend to him all these years, sticking with him even after he had taken her for granted and treated her like his personal assistant or the president of his entourage. He would never do anything to jeopardize their friendship, especially not confess the feelings he'd been having for her for the last several months. She had been head-over-heels in love with him for years in their teens and early twenties, but had been over him for over a decade. His feelings for her now were simply too late.

He scanned the membership app on his phone at the front desk and said hello back to the attendant who greeted him. He walked through the lobby and the free weight area to the back where the locker rooms were and changed out of his crisp button-down oxford and chinos into athletic shorts and a t-shirt. He stowed his stuff in a locker and briefly looked at himself in the mirror before leaving to join his friends.

He had a few grays and a couple of lines on his face, but he pretty much looked the same as he had when he was the king of Cool Springs, back when Rae had a crush on him. He splashed a bit of cold water on his face and told himself to shake it off and not act weird around Rae.

"There's the celebrity now." Byron called out from the sideline as he entered the pickleball courts. "You late because you got held up signing autographs?" His barrel-chested brother-in-law laughed at his own joke.

"Yeah, yeah, let's get out on the court and let's see who's laughing. How much did Rae and I beat you guys by last time?"

Rae, Brisa, Charlie, and Melody stood in a circle talking in the center of the farthest court, so Byron and Gabriel walked over to join them.

"That's not fair," Byron objected. "Get another partner and I bet I can beat you. Hey, why don't you and Brisa partner up and I'll take Rae this time."

Gabriel fake punched Byron's gut. "Brisa's your wife, dude. You can't try to pawn her off on me."

Byron smirked. "Yeah, yeah. I know what's going on. You want Rae all to yourself. Why don't you cut the cute stuff and date that girl? You know you like her."

Gabriel was used to this kind of teasing, especially from Byron. It didn't mean anything. But, as he connected eyes with Rae, he felt a warmth and a quickening of his pulse, and he hoped no one else could tell that after all these years, he'd fallen for his best friend.

"There's my partner. Shall we spot them all a few points to make it fair?" Rae's shoulder-length brown hair was tied into a knot on the top of her head. Gabriel usually loved how her wavy hair framed her petite face, but now he realized that he also loved it all pulled back so that none of her beautiful face was hidden.

"Sounds good, Spencer. Let's also give them first serve."

They got paddles and balls and flipped a coin to see who would play first. Rae and Gabriel lost the coin toss, so Brisa and Byron played Gabriel's other brother-in-law, Charlie, and Rae's friend, Melody.

"Want to warm up?" Rae asked him while the other four started their game.

"Absolutely. I want to mop the floor with these guys." He wriggled his eyebrows up and down, and she laughed, like he knew she would.

Things had changed. When they were kids he flirted with her to boost his ego and to remind Chet that he was winning. Now, he flirted with her just to hear her laugh.

They warmed up on an unoccupied court across the gym from the rest of their group. There were six courts in the large gymnasium and only half were occupied. Over the winter they'd had to sign up for a court and wait until one opened up. The weather had gotten warmer with the coming of spring, so Gabriel guessed the crowds of people who'd been here months ago were now playing outside somewhere.

Rae served, and the two of them volleyed back and forth for a long time, their conversation like the bouncing pickleball, never missing a beat.

"Brisa almost talked me into signing up to be a Sticker

Cutie consultant."

"Don't do it! Stay strong."

"I know. What's your next YouTube video going to be? I've heard the kids are into challenges these days. You thinking about eating a bunch of oranges or waxing all the hair off your face?"

"Um, no. I think I'm going to go back to my old real estate videos for a while, you know, home tours, a little Q and A, educating first home buyers, stuff like that. I'm hoping my audience for the more entertaining stuff will stick with me. What about you? How's old Garner and Fox these days?"

She told him about setting up a temporary office for a visiting engineer and then she told him a couple of funny stories about helping people with their technology issues. In a lot of her stories people usually only needed to turn their computer off and back on, or they hadn't plugged something in.

Gabriel was so proud of her work. She'd always been so quiet and shy when they were younger, and now she was truly a genius when it came to technology, and he'd heard from several people at Garner and Fox that the company relied heavily on her and that the higher ups in the company had taken notice of her and were grooming her for big things. If he knew his friend, though, he would be willing to bet that she had no idea anyone had noticed her, and she didn't see the potential in herself that everyone else saw.

"Guess who I saw this afternoon at the gas station?" She answered her own question before he had a chance to, "Chance Gilmore! He's in town for his brother's wedding."

"Ol Take a Chance!" Gabriel punctuated the nickname of his former basketball teammate while he swatted the pickleball over the net. "I haven't seen that guy in years. Were Monica and the kids with him?"

His old friend had played college basketball in California and met a girl there, got married, and stayed. He was living the west coast life with his growing family, and Gabriel kept up with him sporadically on Facebook.

"They were. He has a beautiful family. He asked about you, and I told him you were doing great."

Gabriel missed the ball and had to jog off court to retrieve it. Was it kind of weird that Chance Gilmore had asked Rae about him? They weren't a couple, never had been, but it seemed everyone thought of them as a pair.

Brisa appeared on the sidelines of their court.

"They're ready for you two. They beat us bad." She fanned herself with her paddle. "I'm going to call the sitter and check on the kids. Your winning streak might be over, little brother, I think Melody's been practicing."

"We aren't scared. Are we, Spencer?"

"Nope!" Rae scooped up her water bottle and bounced off the court to walk next to him. Then she lowered her voice and whispered, "Although it is possible that Melody has improved. She joined one of the league teams and has been playing a lot."

Gabriel wasn't worried. He and Rae had something Melody and Charlie didn't have. They had a history. They'd been best friends for over thirty years.

He assured her that he was fully confident that they would win, and in less than fifteen minutes, they did exactly that.

"Boom Shakka Lakka!" He and Rae chanted in unison. It had been their victory chant since middle school.

"You two kill me," Melody said, out of breath after the match, "You don't even have to use complete sentences to communicate. You just give each other looks or say half a word and know exactly what the other is thinking. That's why no one can beat you." She sunk down in a chair in the corner of the gym and took a long drink out of her water thermos.

"You guys can play us again, if you want." Rae offered. "Let's have a re-match after we play Brisa and Byron."

"You mean after we beat Brisa and Byron." Gabriel corrected her.

Rae swatted his stomach and hushed him. She didn't like trash talk.

Gabriel called out to his sister and brother-in-law who were practicing on the next court, "Oh Byron! Oh Brisa! Come let us embarrass you!"

He loved to trash talk.

Their victory in the next match was even quicker. Everyone wanted to play again, the other players insisting they have another chance to win, but Rae and Gabriel beat them even worse the second time.

After their second loss to Melody and Charlie and their second loss to Rae and Gabriel, Byron and Brisa called it a night, saying they had to get home before their kids' bedtimes.

After they left, Melody had an idea. "Hey, why don't we switch up partners? Rae and I can play against you two? Guys against girls? What do you say?"

Gabriel didn't really want to. Rae had always been his partner. But Charlie wanted to, so he felt compelled to agree, worried that they would all suspect his feelings for Rae if he didn't.

He suggested they spot the women five points – he was trying to be chivalrous, but both women were instantly offended.

After everyone took their place on the court, he whispered to Charlie, "What are we supposed to do? Play them like we'd play a couple of guys? I don't want to be the creeps who embarrassed two girls on the pickleball court."

Charlie answered, "I guess we let them score a few at the beginning so it doesn't look too bad."

Rae served first. The volleys went for several minutes until Melody dinked the ball beautifully over the net right into the front area of the guys' side, the area known as the "kitchen," where it was against the rules to hit the ball. Her hit had been perfect, because it had just enough energy to get the ball over the net and into the kitchen, but not enough to put it into the back court where they could hit it, so the ladies scored the first point.

Charlie and Gabriel looked at each other and shrugged. No big deal. They were going to let them score a few at the beginning anyway.

But then, the next point came when Rae expertly landed a fast-moving ball on Charlie's right side, almost as if she remembered that Charlie was left-handed and intentionally aimed for the area where he would be the slowest to react.

Could she have done that on purpose? Was she that good? Gabriel was starting to wonder if the key to their success hadn't been their partnership but had actually been that Rae was so good?

And then they scored again, and the score was four to zero.

"Have you been letting them score?" Charlie whispered to Gabriel while they were waiting on Rae to serve.

Gabriel shook his head, unable to verbalize that the women

were beating them fair and square.

Finally Melody hit a wild ball, giving the guys the opportunity to serve, and they were able to score a point and then another. Gabriel settled down. Surely the first four points were an anomaly. They'd surely score all the points from here on out.

But he was wrong. It was a long game – twice as long as any other game he'd played that night, and after over thirty minutes the girls won, beating them by three points.

After they won, Rae and Melody bounced to the net, giggling, holding out their hands to shake, but Gabriel didn't want to shake their hands. He knew it was a dumb pickleball game at the community center and meant nothing, but it did mean something. Something he couldn't quite put his finger on.

He put on a smile and shook their hands as if everything was fine, because how could he admit that it bothered him that they beat them?

Rae wasn't a trash talker, but even she couldn't help razzing him and Charlie a little after the victory. Melody seemed to relish the win even more than Rae, and as the four of them exited through the lobby she added insult to injury when she suggested that maybe she and Rae should be partners all of the time.

"That wouldn't work," Charlie responded to her suggestion, "Gabriel couldn't handle it." He laughed as he opened the front glass door for the group.

"What do you mean I couldn't handle it? Rae can play with whomever she wants. I don't care." Why were they acting like he was a needy child? He was a grown man who had a million friends in real life and online and a successful business. Since when was he regarded as the one who desperately needed Rae? "In fact, let's come back Tuesday for a re-match."

Charlie pushed a button on a fob to unlock his red truck and answered, "I'd better not. I probably shouldn't leave Camila home alone with the baby again so soon."

"I can't make it either," Melody shrugged a shoulder as she opened the door to her sleek sports car, "The Jackson Charles Band is playing down at LaFever's that night, and I can't miss it. I missed them the last time they were in town, and I've regretted it ever since. I'll catch you guys next time, though." She told them all goodnight and drove off, the raucous rock music from her car sending vibrations across the parking lot.

"It's a wonder that girl hasn't damaged her hearing." Charlie shook his head at Melody and her music and added that he'd better get home because he'd promised Camila that he'd do the nighttime bottle feeding for baby Caroline, and he didn't want to be late.

"Well, Spencer, looks like you're stuck with me. Does this feel like our school days all over again? Remember when our moms took turns taking us to school every day?"

He knew she hadn't felt stuck with him back then, but was that how she felt now?

She laughed in response. "Oh yes, the carpool." Then she arched one of her perfect dark eyebrows over her intense brown eyes. "Only I never felt stuck with you. There were dozens of girls in school who would've paid money to trade places with me and live next door to the illustrious Gabriel Matthews."

That made him feel slightly better, even though he suspected she was laying it on a little thick to assuage his bruised ego. Still he wanted to ask how she felt now, but of course he couldn't do that, not after years of mistreating her and rubbing Chet's nose in it. No, he would never venture into romance with her now. After all the harm he'd caused, he was lucky she was still willing to be his friend.

They reached her car, and he rested an elbow on the hood while she leaned against the driver's door. It was the usual positions they fell into for a long chat. Gabriel found that he loved these conversations in parking lots, leaning against a car, under a streetlight. Most conversations had a clear purpose – buying or selling a house, making plans with family, checking up on old friends – but these conversations with Rae seemed almost lazy. They didn't really have a point, didn't really go anywhere, but these lazy, pointless parking lot conversations were the most meaningful conversations in his life.

"Sounds like our moms are cooking up a scheme for Mother's Day. Did Evelyn tell you to bring a date and if you didn't, she could set you up?"

"What? Yes, did Lois give you the same challenge?" The two old birds must've come up with the idea over a pot of their chamomile tea.

"Yep, of course she offered it up with a big dollop of guilt on top so I couldn't refuse."

"Lois resorted to guilt? That's not usually her style. I think maybe my mother has been a bad influence on your mother. Maybe we should treat them like two kids who can't get along and separate them?"

She put her hands together and wiggled her fingers deviously. "I say we turn the challenge back around on them. They don't think we can find dates, and that they're going to be able to set us up with someone. I bet my mom already has Dustin Henderson committed to be there. She's been trying to set us up for years."

"Dustin Henderson? Wasn't he in middle school when we were seniors? Doesn't he manage Fresh Market?" He shot her a lopsided grin. "I mean, who could resist a younger man who could keep you stocked in fresh produce?"

"I have no interest in Dustin, and my mom knows that. She keeps hoping I'll change my mind, though. I'm sure she has a cinematic meet cute planned for me to enter her house on Mother's Day and see him and fall in love. What she doesn't expect is for me to bring a date."

She spoke as if she had a plan, and for a minute, Gabriel thought she was going to propose they go together. He almost wished she would. What if they could pretend like the past never happened, that they'd just met each other and could go on a date like normal people who had feelings for each other? Although, it seemed he was the only one who had romantic feelings in this relationship. Hers were long gone.

After an awkward second, she continued.

"Let's help each other find dates! Neither of us have tried online dating, and everyone is doing it now. What do you think? I can help you create a profile that women would respond to, and you can help me?"

Her sweet eyes were bright over her hopeful smile, as if she'd discovered a plan to make both of their mothers happy. How could he tell her that he wished they could accomplish that with a much simpler solution?

Chapter Five

Rae looked at the clock on the wall in the temporary office she was setting up for the environmental engineer from Georgia. Eleven-thirty. She was nearly done here, and then she could leave at noon. She looked forward to getting her garden in after work. She had tilled the small ten by ten area in her back yard and prepared the ground several days ago, so now she was ready to plant. She planned to plant her usual tomatoes, kale, and peppers, but this year she would forego squash since she hadn't had any luck with it the last few years and was attempting green beans instead.

She stood and dusted her hands and surveyed her work. A fully connected laptop sat centered on the desk, ready for Mr. Stayton to use. The office was clean and functional, albeit devoid of personality with a black desk chair, white standing desk, two matching gray visitor chairs, and three blank walls; the fourth wall's only decoration was the digital clock with glowing green numbers.

"Hello? I think this is where I'm supposed to be?"

Rae looked up. A man who looked like a hero in a romantic comedy movie stood in the doorway. A perfect set of white teeth and the outline of chiseled biceps perceptible under his knit polo – not exactly what she expected in an environmental engineer.

"Hello!" She crossed the room with a hand extended to shake. "You must be Carter Stayton. I'm Rae from IT. Your office is all set up and ready to go." She shook his hand and continued, feeling a little shaky at his appearance. "Your password is just GarnerandFox with a capital G and a capital F and no spaces, and it'll prompt you to make up a new password when you sign in. Printer is right across the hall, and you're connected. Wi-fi and everything should be working great. I emailed you the pathway to the company drive. Email, call or text me if you have any troubles. My contact info is in the personnel file on the drive."

She dried her sweaty palms on her business casual pants,

hoping she didn't sound too flustered. He was the type of person who was obviously good looking, the type of person who probably got offered modeling contracts while in public places.

"Thanks, ah, ma'am." He put his hand out as if to shake hers and then pulled it back to his side as if embarrassed that he'd considered shaking her hand.

Mr. Ellis entered the room behind him and clapped him on the back.

"Oh good, you two have met." Mr. Ellis pushed his round wire-rimmed glasses up his nose and examined the room. "Everything ship-shape in here, Rae?"

"Yes, sir. He's ready to go."

"Thank you both." Mr. Stayton crossed to the desk and opened his new laptop, without making eye contact with either of them. "The commission meeting about the Phillips project is on Tuesday, so I'd better get to work."

"Of course." Rae went to the door to get out of the way since he seemed intent on getting started with his work.

"Just a minute, Rae." Mr. Ellis stopped her. "Carter, you've got a lot to do, but let us welcome you. Can we treat you to dinner tonight?"

He furrowed his eyebrows at something on his computer screen, shook his head, and answered without looking up, "That's very kind of you, Dennis, but I'll just order something in. I really have a lot to do."

"Studies actually show an uptick in productivity after a break for nourishment and socialization," Mr. Ellis persuaded. "An hour. It'll do you good to get your mind off of it for an hour. There's a great barbeque restaurant less than a mile away."

Carter Stayton looked up from his computer. The stress wrinkles across his perfect forehead relaxed and he nodded at Mr. Ellis.

"Okay, I'll take you up on it. Can we meet at seven? I should be ready for a break by then."

"Affirmative, I'll send you the address." Mr. Ellis stepped into the hall with Rae and shut the office door. Then he whispered to Rae, "I won't be able to be at dinner."

Rae's chin dropped.

He reached into his pocket and pulled out a credit card and

handed it to her.

"Take my company card and have a nice meal with Carter Stayton. He's single and approximately your age. The two of you would be a lovely couple, don't you think?" His nose twitched and his cheeks turned pink.

Was her boss setting her up? First her mom and now her boss. Did she have a label across her forehead that said, "Pathetic"?

"Mr. Ellis, I, ah, I don't know what to say." She wanted to tell him that Carter Stayton had fumbled a handshake and hadn't looked her in the eye during their entire interaction, so she doubted there would be fireworks between them.

He shrugged his narrow shoulders and swallowed, his Adam's apple going up and down his thin neck. "Go enjoy some barbeque and have a conversation. Maybe something will come of it, and maybe something won't. You've got a fifty percent chance of it working out if you try, but a zero percent chance if you don't."

She'd never thought of Mr. Ellis as profound, but he was right. She needed to take more chances. She should give it a shot.

"And if it doesn't work out, then at least I get some free barbeque, right?"

"Exactly," he acted relieved, but then added, "just don't go overboard."

"Of course not, sir."

She headed to her office to get her things and get out of the building before anyone could catch her and ask for help. She wanted to get outside, away from technology and people, and get her hands in the soil. On her way to the stairwell, Melody joined her. She started talking mid-sentence, like she always did, because their life had become one ongoing conversation.

She had two different concerts she planned to attend that weekend. Naturally. The woman loved music more than anyone Rae had ever known. After rattling down her list of planned activities for the weekend, she asked Rae what she had planned.

"Of course, church on Sunday. On Saturday morning I'm supposed to help Gabriel babysit Byron and Brisa's three kids." She stuck out her tongue in fake exhaustion. "I'm also really hoping to get my garden all planted, and ah, well," she paused, kind of embarrassed to admit she had a Mr. Ellis-set-up-date tonight, "tonight I'm taking a visiting engineer out for dinner for Mr. Ellis." She hoped the set-up part of the dinner wasn't obvious.

Melody stopped mid-step and threw a hand on Rae's arm.

"Hold up. Is the visiting engineer Carter Stayton, because Oh. My. Goodness."

She couldn't keep a giggle from escaping. She felt like a teenager gossiping about a cute boy, but Melody was right – Carter Stayton was "Oh. My. Goodness." gorgeous.

"It is him! Rae Spencer, you are the luckiest woman in the universe. I saw him walking through the lobby and asked someone who the visiting movie star was. That blonde hair and square jaw and body builder physique? Like I said, Oh. My. Goodness."

Rae laughed again at her friend's dramatics and tried to downplay her dinner.

"It's nothing more than a business dinner. He said he was super busy, so I'm sure it'll be quick. Mr. Ellis even set it up," she added.

The two women reached the bottom floor and crossed the lobby to exit to the parking lot, both in a hurry to escape to their weekend. Rae was mildly excited about her dinner. He was good looking, but she didn't even know him, and they hadn't exactly clicked in their first meeting.

Once outside, Melody slid her aviator sunglasses on her face and tilted her head at Rae.

"How do you think your BFF Gabriel will react to you dating someone?"

Rae waved her question off. "One business dinner on the company card doesn't qualify as dating, but I've dated lots of people, and he's totally fine with it." She paused and thought about it and then corrected herself, "Well, I haven't exactly dated lots of people. I've dated some people, and he's always been fine with it." Then she thought again, thinking of the paltry number of men she'd dated – Man, maybe she did have the word pathetic written across her forehead.

"Okay, the truth is, I haven't dated much. I have dated some, but not a lot, but Gabriel doesn't care. He isn't bothered at all by my dating, and why should he be? He dates lots of women, and I've never had a problem with it. Why would he care if I'm dating someone?"

And even though Rae was posing the question, deep down she really knew why Melody asked. Of course, she knew. Melody asked because Rae pretended to not be bothered when Gabriel was dating people, but she was bothered . . . greatly bothered. Where she had dated a handful of people her entire life, he had dated dozens, maybe even hundreds of women. But, strangely, all of that stopped when his dad died nine months ago. The guy who had multiple dates a week with different women and who had been through a series of monogamous relationships had suddenly stopped dating altogether, and Rae had no idea why.

Melody put both hands on Rae's shoulders and looked at her over the tops of her glasses. "Listen, I think Gabriel is incredible. Maybe even good enough for you. Maybe." She leaned closer to Rae and continued, "But, he's had a million girlfriends and you always on the side as his bestie. I think he's been spoiled. Maybe you've been a bit too available. Maybe he'll appreciate you more if you are suddenly busy with a good-looking environmental engineer from Georgia?"

Melody winked at her and said goodbye, and Rae wished her a fun and relaxing weekend. After her friend got in her car, Rae took a moment to look at the big blue sky and breathe in the spring air. She could smell the beginnings of green grass and trees. The long winter was officially over, and she couldn't wait to get to her backyard garden.

She arrived at her three-bedroom brick house and smiled at the dandelions and purple nettles in her front yard as she pulled into the garage. She changed into a pair of comfy yoga pants, since it wasn't quite warm enough for shorts, and a t-shirt that read, 'Sometimes I wet my plants' and headed to her favorite place in the world, her backyard.

She had fallen in love with the 1980's ranch style home and bought it four years ago. With its brick exterior and light blue shutters and white columns on the front porch, it was everything she wanted in a home. She'd lived in apartments and rent houses until she was twenty-nine and decided it was time to invest in a house.

She took everything she needed to the garden space she'd created behind her house and began planting kale. As she sowed the seeds into the soil in rows, she thought about what Melody had said. Had she been too available to Gabriel? Did he take her for granted because she'd always been there?

As she finished up the kale and started planting tomato plants, she thought about their conversation in the parking lot the night before. She had tried to insinuate that they should turn the tables on their mothers by going together, but Gabriel hadn't caught on. When he didn't say anything, she had hurriedly suggested that they help each other find dates. Even though it had happened the night before, and she was now alone in her garden, she shuddered with embarrassment at how she'd thought he would get the hint and agree to go with her. How embarrassing. She'd never do that again.

It had been the second time that evening that she'd been horribly embarrassed. The first was at the gas station when she saw Chance Gilmore, or Ol' Take a Chance, as Gabriel always called him. She'd been the first to see him – standing at the gas pump, his seven-foot frame impossible to miss. The instant she realized who it was, she shut off the gas pump and snapped the fuel door shut on her car as fast as she could, but she wasn't fast enough. He'd seen her and was walking over to say hello.

The basketball star was kind and didn't let on that he remembered what had happened at his house their senior year. Although, the more Rae thought about it the more she realized he had to have been pretending not to remember. How could anyone forget how desperate she'd been that night? And then it all got worse the next day when they realized that Chet was missing.

She tried to remind herself that it was all in the past. Ancient history.

But some things just stick with you. Even though it had almost been twenty years ago, she still felt like the girl who had embarrassingly flung herself at Gabriel Matthews. She still felt like the girl whose other best friend had disappeared the next day. Her dear friend whom she'd known since childhood had vanished, and to this day no one knew whether he'd been kidnapped or had run away. The police hadn't found anything. Private investigators hired by the Donnellys hadn't found anything. Chet was simply gone.

And now she and Gabriel could only ever be friends, even

though she loved him completely. The thought of helping him find a date made her stomach turn. What was she supposed to do? Go door to door looking for a woman for him? Help him set up an online dating profile? Was he planning on setting her up with one of his friends? She just couldn't do it.

She stabbed at the ground viciously with her trowel, taking her frustration out on the dirt, and then she stopped. She had an idea.

What if Carter Stayton were her Mother's Day date?

It was perfect. He was only going to be in town for a month. He checked all of the boxes: looks, intelligence, success. He was the type of man she could bring as her date and no one would compare him to Gabriel. No one would feel sorry for her that Gabriel hadn't chosen her. Let's be honest. With Carter Stayton, it wouldn't matter if Gabriel brought a NASA astronaut who was also a beauty queen, she would still win.

If only she could convince him to come with her.

She finished planting and cleaned up her mess and then looked at her hands. They were satisfyingly dirty. She went back inside the house through the patio door that entered her kitchen and looked at her wall clock that was in the shape of a sunflower. It had been her grandmother's. It was a few minutes after six. She was going to have to hurry to make it to the restaurant by seven.

She showered, partially dried her hair with a hair dryer, and then applied make-up. She had never been a full-face-of-make-up type of person. But she did have a quirk about her eyebrows and her lipstick. She liked to keep her dark brows neatly shaped and a deep red color on her lips.

She put on a long, flowy dress that she felt especially pretty and confident in and looked at herself in her bathroom mirror. Not too bad. She thought she was pretty.

Why didn't Gabriel agree?

Maybe Carter Stayton would see her differently than Gabriel saw her.

She drove to the barbeque restaurant Mr. Ellis had picked for the dinner and parallel parked on the street in front. As she locked her car doors, she winced at the giant pink pig that hung over the front door of the establishment. If she'd had a say in it, she would have picked a different place.

Loud country music assaulted her ears as soon as she opened the front door. She'd never been a fan of the twangy music or its constant references to beer, dogs, trucks, and women, but she was definitely out-voted on that subject in her hometown where it seemed everyone else loved Reba and Garth and Carrie.

She stepped into the lobby and was greeted by a cowboy hat wearing host who shouted over the country music that the wait for a table would be twenty-five minutes, and she sat on a bench to wait for Carter. She pulled out her phone to busy herself until he arrived. She had three missed texts from Gabriel.

Text number one was sent at six thirty-five:
Gabriel
Do you remember what kind of berry I'm allergic to?

Text number two was sent at six forty-three:
Gabriel
Remember we're supposed to babysit for B&B tomorrow. They're going to Fresh Market. Can you imagine having so many kids that you have to buy groceries in bulk?

Text number three was sent at six fifty-seven:
Gabriel
I was asking about the berries because I was thinking about trying an acai bowl. I've never had one, but I've heard they're good. Have you had one?

She shook her head at him and started to respond that he was allergic to raspberries (how could he not remember that?), when the gorgeous Carter Stayton entered the restaurant.

He smiled at her and nodded.

"Hello, Carter, not sure if you remember me, I'm Rae Spencer," she said brightly and held out her hand for him to shake. She wanted to smack herself in the forehead. Of course he remembered her. They met only seven hours ago.

"Of course, nice to see you again." He politely shook her hand and then looked around and grimaced and asked, "Is it loud in here or is that just me?"

"It's not just you. It's definitely loud. Are you a country music fan?"

"No." He said without hesitation. "I'm into indie rock."

"Oh really? You should meet my friend, Melody, she's a huge indie rock fan. She goes to like four concerts a week." She looked around the pig-themed restaurant and asked, "Are you a fan of barbeque?"

He shrugged apologetically. "Sorry, but no. I hope I don't sound overly negative." He sighed and rubbed the bridge of his nose like he was trying to ease a headache. "I appreciate you and Dennis showing me hospitality, but I really have a lot of work to do. Do you think we can go ahead and take a seat and order so I can get back to the office as soon as possible? Would Dennis mind if we ordered for him?"

Rae could feel heat rush to her cheeks. She hoped he wouldn't realize that Dennis' absence was actually part of his set-up plan for the two of them.

"Dennis actually couldn't make it, so it's just the two of us. I'm not a big fan of barbeque myself. How about we go somewhere else? There are several options on this block." When she saw him look at his watch, she added, "We could even get something to-go that you could take back to the office."

His perfect face looked a little sheepish. "Sorry. I don't mean to be bad company. I've got to do about six months' worth of work in a month, so that's all I can think about."

"Not a problem." She pulled the strap of her purse over her shoulder went to the exit. "What kind of food do you like? On this block there's a pizza place, a sandwich shop, a health food café, and a sushi bar." Out on the sidewalk she looked up at him and smiled, "Any of those sound good?"

He picked the health food café, and Rae wasn't surprised. She assumed his good looks didn't come from a diet of burgers and pizza. They walked three doors down to The Flower Café and ordered carry-out meals from the counter. Then they sat in bar stools at the juice bar while they waited on their food.

"Have you been to Oklahoma before?" She had been trying to think of a conversation starter, and that lame question was all she could think of.

He nodded. "Yes, my grandparents live here."

Ah. She pressed her lips together and nodded.

"Near Tulsa." He added.

Interesting. So far, their conversation was less than riveting. She would have to up her game if she wanted him to come to her mom's house for Mother's Day.

"Do you play pickleball?" It was all she could think of.

He shook his head. "No." He drummed his fingers on the bar. "I play basketball in a league at our community center, though."

"Oh, basketball. I played basketball in high school." Dear Lord, she wished she could think about something else to say about basketball.

He smiled and nodded again. This was dreadful.

Oh! She thought of something to say about basketball.

"Do you like the Thunder?"

He smiled. "I do. I love the Thunder. We don't have any pro teams in Georgia, of course, so I've adopted them as my own. Do you like them?"

He tilted his gorgeous head to the side like he was truly interested, and Rae got distracted by his face for a second. How could any human be that good looking?

"Um, ahem, yes. I do. I like the Thunder. I keep up with them, anyway. I don't get to go to very many games, but I watch them on TV and keep up."

Now it was his turn to press his lips together and nod.

She decided to dive in and ask.

"So, Mother's Day is next week. Think you'll be going back to Georgia to see your mom?"

He wrinkled his eyebrows at her, as if perplexed why a stranger would be asking if he had plans for Mother's Day, of all holidays.

The waitress delivered their bagged meals before he answered, and he stood as soon as he had his roasted Brussels sprouts and sweet potatoes in hand.

"Thank you for paying for my dinner, and sorry to rush off, but I really do have a lot to get done."

She waved off his apology and stood next to him. "No problem, at all. The company paid for the meal. I hope you enjoy your time in Cool Springs, and let me know if you need anything."

He walked out of the café, and she followed. Well, that was that. Not only were there no sparks, there wasn't even a hint of a flicker. They could barely think of a handful of words to say to each other. She would have to come up with another idea for a Mother's Day date.

Back out on the sidewalk, he told her that he was walking back to the office and she told him that her car was parked across the street. He thanked her again, and she told him to have a nice night.

They turned to go their separate ways. Rae was across the street with her hand on the handle of her car when she heard her name behind her.

"Rae!"

She turned to see Carter Stayton jogging across the street to her.

"I am sorry that I'm not much of a conversationalist. I tend to make friends with people who are extroverted talkers, so I don't have to talk very much."

He looked down at his shoes, and Rae realized something. Carter Stayton, the world's most beautiful human, was shy.

He cleared his throat and looked up at her. "And I think you might be a bit like me, perhaps?"

She thought about the dynamics of her relationship with Gabriel, aka the definition of "extroverted talker."

"Maybe we should introduce ourselves again." She held a hand out for him to shake. "I'm the pot, and you must be the kettle."

He laughed.

"Let's try this again sometime, but let's go to an actual restaurant and sit at a table." He fiddled with the plastic bag in his hand and then continued, "I don't know anyone here, and if I'm going to be here for a month it would be nice to have a, well, to make a, um, you know, a friend."

She blinked, taking in his hesitation and the words he did – and didn't – say.

He looked down at the plastic bag in his hands as if he'd never seen a plastic bag before.

Rae finally found her voice. "That sounds nice. Maybe you can text me the details?"

They parted awkwardly, and Rae got into her car and started it. She wanted to call Gabriel. She wanted to discuss her strange dinner with him and ask what he thought about it, but at the same time she didn't want to tell him. She wanted to tell him, because he was the person she told all of her news. It had been months since she'd had a date, and so even a possibility of a future date was news. In the past, she always told him about her dates, but it was different now. He hadn't dated anyone in so long that it seemed like he'd made her "his person" even more than before, and she had loved every minute of it. But what were they? Were they still just friends? They'd never kissed or held hands. He'd never even put an arm around her.

So why didn't she feel like she could tell him about Carter Stayton?

She drove home and turned on a true crime documentary and ate her take-out avocado Caesar salad. Her mom sent her a game notification for their favorite phone game, and Rae beat her three times in a row. She was about to accept another challenge from her mom, when a call came through. It was Gabriel.

She declined her mom's challenge and accepted his call.

"Have you ever had an acai bowl?"

"I have not. Was it good?" She settled back into her oversized plush armchair and got comfortable for one of their talks.

"So good. You'd like it. I'm taking you sometime this week. Maybe after we babysit tomorrow? Did I tell you what I had to do tonight? Where were you tonight, by the way? I drove by earlier, and it looked like you weren't home."

This was talking with Gabriel. She decided to skip the topic of where she was and concentrate on the acai bowls.

"What do they taste like?"

"What does what taste like?" He paused. "Oh, acai bowls? So good. Kind of like fruity ice cream, but better. I went to a place over in Moore with Robby York. Remember him? Well, he's thinking about putting in a health food café that serves acai bowls here in Cool Springs and is trying to get me to invest. What do you think? Do you think our small town could support another health food café? You've been to that one by your office, haven't you?"

She thought about her uncomfortable evening with Carter Stayton.

"Yes, I've been there. It didn't look very busy."

"Hmm. Well, I think Robby is doing some market research. We'll have to look at the numbers. Did you get your garden planted?"

She didn't think she'd told him about finishing her garden. Had she?

"I did. How did you know that? Have you got a hidden camera in my backyard?"

"Yes! I've got them all over your house, Spencer, so I know when I can sneak over and steal your collection of state spoons!"

She howled in laughter. "How did you know I have a collection of state spoons?"

"How did I know? I don't remember how I originally found out, but how could I forget? Who under the age of eighty has a spoon collection?"

"They're not just any spoons. They're state spoons. A spoon from every state."

He laughed at her. "Oh well, now that you say that it makes perfect sense. Totally normal."

She snorted. "Shut up. You don't know how to buy lightbulbs. Bulbs go out in your home and you just keep them there, dark and dead, until you can't see, and then you go buy like fifty bulbs at once."

He was quiet on the other end for a moment.

"I don't know how to buy lightbulbs? I don't know how to *buy lightbulbs*?" He repeated incredulously. "Spencer, you are a really terrible trash talker."

She giggled. He was right. She wasn't very good with cut-downs.

"Seriously, Gabriel, how did you know I was finishing my garden? I don't think I said anything to you about it, and you're not exactly the gardening type." That was an understatement. Gabriel's fingernails were straighter and cleaner than hers.

"It's mid-May. You always put in a garden around this time of year. You always say that you try to finish it by the beginning of the month, but every year you say that you're a week behind. I know you, Spencer, you love getting outside when the weather starts getting warmer. You put on a pair of yoga pants and a t-shirt with a funny saying on it, and you go outside for hours working in your garden, re-painting your shed, planting flowers, making little pieces of garden art out of stuff you found in the trash. Then, after you're finished, and your hands are good and dirty, your cheeks are bright red, and you look happier than you have in months."

Something caught in Rae's throat. She couldn't respond. How could a person know another person so well?

On the other end of the line, Gabriel cleared his throat.

"Anyway, that's how I figured you probably finished your garden today."

Chapter Six

"Maaa-oooomm! Daaa-aad! Uncle Gabriel and Rae are here!"

Brinley's high-pitched scream on the other side of the front door greeted Gabriel and Rae when they stepped on the porch.

"Think it's too late to run? Tell them we forgot? Byron and Brisa can take their little beasts to the store with them." He turned back toward the driveway, but Rae grabbed his arm and turned him back around.

"Oh no you don't. They've already seen us."

Gabriel groaned. He loved his nephew and nieces, but they were a lot of work. Actually, to be more accurate, his nieces, Bella and Brinley, were a lot of work. His nephew, Beckham, was no trouble at all. At eleven, he was a perfect little gentleman. Bella and Brinley, the six-year-old twins, were a pair of freckle-faced, pig-tail wearing tornadoes.

The front door swung open and smacked into the wall behind it. Brinley, one half of the terrible two, stood at the door wearing a cowgirl hat, a princess costume, a pink tutu and boots.

"Can we play Horses and Ice Cream, Uncle Gabriel? Pleeeeaaasseee?" She smiled up at them revealing a new gap on her top row of teeth.

"I don't know. Does your sister want to play? Remember the rule we made last time? I'll only play if you agree and take turns."

Horses and Ice Cream was a made-up game he'd been playing with the girls since they were three. It basically consisted of him acting like a horse and the girls riding him to the ice cream parlor, where they pretended to eat double scoops of chocolate ice cream. On the way to the ice cream parlor, Uncle Gabriel the Horse often took wrong turns and gently bucked them off and got distracted from the journey, and Bella and Brinley had to remind him where they were going. He wondered how much longer they would want to play the game. It was sad to think they'd probably outgrow it soon.

"Bella!" Brinley shouted with the full force of her lungs, "Want to play Horses and Ice Cream?"

She ran off, presumably to find her twin, and Rae and Gabriel entered the chaotic house.

They walked through the living room around piles of folded laundry to the kitchen where Brisa greeted them with a nod, but without a word. She had her phone to her ear and appeared to be in the middle of something serious. Beckham sat at the table eating a bowl of cereal. Gabriel sat next to him at the table, and Rae went to the cabinet and got a mug and then poured herself a cup of coffee from Brisa's Mr. Coffee.

"What's up, little man?" Gabriel greeted his nephew. "What do you have on the agenda today?"

Beckham slurped a spoonful of cereal and shrugged. "Just hanging out here. I've got baseball practice this afternoon, but that's it all day. Landon has a new dirt bike, so I might go next door and check it out."

A shiver of fear arrested Gabriel's heart for a moment. A dirt bike? Beckham wasn't old enough for that, was he? Couldn't he get hurt on a dirt bike?

"I want to go over there with you if you go while I'm here." Then he added quickly so Beckham wouldn't realize he was nervous about him on a dirt bike, "You know, I just want to check it out too."

"Sure, Uncle Gabriel."

"Cool." Then, Gabriel tried to add nonchalantly, "Landon does have a helmet, right?"

Beckham smiled at his uncle.

"Are you scared I'm going to hurt myself, Uncle Gabriel? Because I've ridden dirt bikes lots of times. In fact, dad even said he might get me one for my birthday."

"Might get you one – might. Emphasis on the word, "might," Brisa held the phone away from her face and stage whispered to them.

Rae settled into a stool at the bar next to the table with her coffee mug, cradling the mug in her hands as if the warm substance inside was giving her life. She must be powering up for the next two hours.

Byron entered the room hefting a laundry basket filled full of folded towels.

"Morning guys! Thanks for coming over. I'm going to finish putting up all the laundry, and then Brisa and I will head out." He sat the basket on the bar for a second and rested his roundish dad belly on top of the towels. "She's arguing with our health insurance. They're saying they won't pay for Brinley's trip to the emergency room last month because we went to a hospital that wasn't covered by our insurance. Can you believe that?"

Brisa, the ultimate multi-tasking mom, was now emptying the dishwasher while lecturing the insurance representative over the phone. Gabriel had no doubt that Brisa would be successful in convincing the insurance company to cover the claim. Brisa may not have gone to law school, but he had complete confidence that his bulldog eldest sister could argue any side of any case before the supreme court and win.

Double Trouble appeared in the kitchen and began demanding in unison, "Horses and Ice Cream! Horses and Ice Cream! Horses and Ice Cream!"

Rae smirked at him over the rim over her mug. "Your adoring fans are waiting, Uncle Gabriel."

He groaned. "Okay, girls. The horse is coming."

The twins cheered as he got on all fours. They climbed onto his back, and one of them ordered, "Go to the ice cream store, Horsey!"

Uncle Gabriel the Horse carried the girls throughout the house, obeying every order they shouted at him. They giggled as he bumped into doorways and took wrong turns and neighed loudly. By the time they got to the kitchen, which they all agreed was the ice cream parlor, Brisa and Byron had left for the grocery store and Rae and Beckham were playing a game on the Xbox in the living room.

He convinced Brinley and Bella to give the horse a rest, because his knees were worn out, and agreed to attend a tea party in their bedroom.

"Sure, you two go get everything all set up, and then I'll join you." He settled onto the couch wincing a little when he bent his sore knees.

The tiny tornadoes agreed and went into their bedroom to set up the tea party, and Gabriel leaned back on the couch and closed his eyes.

"Is the horsey tired?" Rae asked.

He opened his eyes. She was focused on the screen where she and Beckham were playing a racing game.

"How did I get assigned to playing with the twins and you get to play video games with Beckham?"

Rae shrugged and kept her eyes on the game, but Beckham answered his question.

"Rae's really good at video games, Uncle Gabriel, and the twins like you, so you know, it just works out."

Gabriel snorted at his nephew. He knew the real story. The truth was that Beckham had always had a little crush on Rae.

A high-pitched voice from down the hall called out, "Uncle Gabriel! It's time for our tea party!"

Gabriel played along as Brinley and Bella served him imaginary tea, and continued playing with them when they wanted to switch to coloring. He was sitting cross-legged with them on the floor of their bedroom coloring a picture of a ballerina when Rae stuck her head in the room.

"Anybody getting hungry for lunch?"

"Yes!" Gabriel and the girls answered her in unison.

Rae chuckled.

Her quiet chuckle was another of his favorite laughs of hers. She did it often, but it never got old. It was low and breathy, a mere hint of a laugh, but he loved it.

"How about ham and cheese sandwiches?" She offered.

The girls cheered for sandwiches, and they all headed to the kitchen to help. In the midst of each child selecting their cheese and mustard or mayo, wheat or white for their sandwich, Gabriel remembered his mom's challenge and Rae's offer to help. It wasn't what he wanted. He wished he could just ask Rae to go as his date, and everything would be smooth and easy, but he knew that would be impossible.

Besides, he knew he had a problem with romantic relationships. No one dated as many people as he did without having some sort of issue with commitment. He was self-aware enough to admit that to himself, so he knew any romantic relationship with Rae would eventually end. He would find some way to make it tank. Even though he wished it wasn't true, he knew that he would sabotage it and then the friendship would be over as well.

And he could not let that happen. He would not let that happen. Their friendship meant the world to him. So, instead, he would ask her to help him find a date.

Made sense, right?

"Do you think you could help me with that thing while the kids eat their sandwiches?" He asked covertly, not wanting the little ears to know what he was talking about.

"That thing?" Rae asked as she pulled juice boxes out of the refrigerator.

"You know, the thing we talked about the other night?" He hoped she would get it before Beckham figured out what he was saying. He didn't want his nephew to think he couldn't find a date on his own. He helped the twins get into their chairs at the table and went to the refrigerator when they asked for grapes.

"Remember, helping me to set up . . . you know." He got the grapes out and gave them to the girls.

"Set up?" She looked puzzled.

He was going to have to say it.

He leaned close to her ear and whispered, "An online dating profile, remember?"

"Online dating?" Beckham announced from his seat at the table. "You're going to do online dating, Uncle Gabriel?"

The kid had ears like a CIA bug.

Rae raised an ornery eyebrow at him. She knew what he meant the whole time.

Gabriel turned his attention to his nephew. "Yeah, it's just for fun. Like you and video games."

"I don't think it's like video games at all, Uncle Gabriel." The kid sat frozen over his lunch, not falling for anything.

"No, of course it's not like video games. I don't know why I said that." He scratched the back of his neck, suddenly feeling very embarrassed and awkward.

Rae handed him a ham and cheddar on wheat and then responded to Beckham. "Online dating is a way to meet new people, and there's nothing wrong with that. If your uncle can find a nice woman to spend time with through it, that would be a good thing, don't you think?"

"But," Beckham tilted his head and wrinkled his nose. "Why does he need to find a nice woman to spend time with when he already has you?"

Gabriel cleared his throat. The kid had a point, and he had no idea how to answer. It wasn't as if he could explain to his eleven-year-old nephew the complexities involved in his and Rae's relationship.

Thankfully, Rae answered for them both. "He does already have me as his friend, but he's looking for something more than that." She sat next to Beckham at the table and pulled out her phone. "He is looking for a girlfriend, you know, someone he can kiss and hold hands with and maybe one day marry."

Beckham's jaw dropped and his eyes bugged. "Uncle Gabriel wants to get *married*?"

Gabriel stepped forward and held out a hand. "Woah, woah, wait a minute. I just said I was looking for a date to the Mother's Day lunch. No one said anything about getting married."

"Well, not right away, but eventually." Rae attempted to explain.

Gabriel didn't know how to respond. Sure, marriage was the standard path, the normal culmination of the happily ever after, but he had no idea how that would work for him. He'd never had a relationship with a woman that had lasted longer than about a year. Well, except with Rae, of course.

"Let's stop all of the marriage talk and just find me a date for one lunch, okay?"

Rae laughed good-naturedly. "Calm down, Gabriel. We aren't calling the preacher yet. Come look at this." She waved him over to look at her phone. "Melody told me about this dating app. She said it had the least amount of crazies on it."

He crossed the kitchen and stood behind Rae's chair and leaned over to look over her shoulder at her phone and got momentarily distracted by how good her hair smelled – like peppermint.

Rae pulled up his headshot from his realtor's website. "Is this picture okay to use for your profile?"

"Sure, it's fine, I guess."

"Wait a minute." Beckham sat his sandwich down on the table. "Let me see it."

Rae turned her phone around so he could see.

"Oh no, Uncle Gabriel. You look like you want to sell something. You need a picture that makes you look like a fun guy. I thought you had game."

Did the child who it seemed was just born yesterday actually accuse him of not having game?

"You thought I had game? You thought I had game?" Gabriel jumped over to his nephew and picked him up over his head in a wrestling-style move. "Boy, your uncle has game! Don't you ever act like I don't have game or I'll have to tickle you until you can't breathe."

Beckham was laughing, and his little sisters who sat at the table with their sandwiches started laughing too.

"Tickle him! Tickle him!" Bella started chanting and then Brinley joined her.

Gabriel laid Beckham down on the couch and started tickling him mercilessly. When the boy finally apologized and admitted that his uncle had game, Gabriel finally let up.

Rae found a picture of Gabriel from a ski trip that Beckham said was acceptable, and then the three of them worked together on his profile. Gabriel felt like a pathetic project. How did it come to this? For years, he had women lined up waiting to date him, but now he had to rely on his best friend and his nephew to catch a woman for him? Sheesh.

"Why don't we set one of these profiles up for you?" He asked Rae. Maybe they could shift the focus to her singleness and it would make him feel less pathetic.

"Um," she bit her lower lip, "I'm not sure if I need one."

"What do you mean? You've got the same deal with your mom, and Mother's Day is in eight days."

Suddenly she seemed very interested in a loose thread on the hem of her shirt.

"Hang on. Do you have a date already?" How had he missed it?

She shrugged and didn't look at him. "I'm not sure yet, but there is this guy who's, well, he's a possibility."

A possibility? How had this happened without him

knowing? He knew everything about Rae. He watched her mess with her shirt uncomfortably, and his heart ached. She had a possibility, and it wasn't him.

Hours later, after sandwiches, more playing the part of a "horsey," watching the next-door neighbor ride his dirt bike, and saying an awkward goodbye to Rae, Gabriel strapped on a pair of boxing gloves and unleashed his frustration on a punching bag at the community center. Even though he pounded the daylights out of the bag, it didn't help. He'd already maxed out on bench press and sprinted a mile on the treadmill, but nothing had given him relief.

Rae had a "possibility."

Who was this guy? Someone she met when she went out with Melody a couple of weeks ago? Someone from church? Someone she met at work? One of her neighbors? What if he wasn't a good guy? What if he was trying to scam her out of her money, or what if he was planning on hurting her?

He needed to punch the bag some more.

As he rhythmically boxed, an image of a fictional guy who represented Rae's possibility manifested on the leather bag. Gabriel envisioned himself beating the dude's face to a bloody pulp.

Until a spring broke and the leather bag went flying across the gym.

Laughter and applause broke out among the weightlifters and people working out. Gabriel's face went red and he lifted a hand to wave at all of them good-naturedly.

"Got a little rage problem tonight, bro?"

His brother-in-law, Charlie, appeared with a backpack on his shoulders.

Gabriel laughed, (because what else was he supposed to do?), and then went to retrieve the broken punching bag.

"Want to go to one of those rage rooms? I've never been, but I've heard they give you a sledgehammer and let you break glass and pulverize a car." Charlie grinned under his firefighter mustache. "I'm not saying I have rage, but after three months of no sleep, breaking things with no consequences sounds very appealing."

"Baby still not sleeping?" Gabriel asked sympathetically.

Charlie and Camila's newborn daughter, Caroline, was their first child, and she had rocked their world.

"Oh sure, she sleeps during the day, but at night she's ready to party. And by party, I mean scream her head off."

Charlie did look tired. Gabriel guessed his firefighter brother-in-law secretly cherished his nights on call at the fire station.

"Seriously, though. Everything okay?"

Gabriel knew that Charlie asked out of sincerity. He'd married Camila nearly ten years ago, so he felt like a real brother. They'd spent a lot of time together on family outings and often hung out. Charlie had been a friend to Gabriel through the loss of his dad. But, Gabriel hadn't told him about his feelings for Rae. He'd never told anyone about that. Now, after all these years, it was embarrassing to admit to anyone, even Charlie, that he had changed his mind and that he actually did have romantic feelings toward the girl that he'd sworn for years to have no feelings for after she had already gotten over her feelings for him.

"Everything's fine. Just, you know, work stuff." Gabriel lied.

"Work stuff has you murdering punching bags? Sure it doesn't have anything to do with your mother's challenge and Rae?"

"How did you – "

"How did I know that one day you'd fall for that girl and when you did fall it would be hard? Hmm, let me think," Charlie stroked his mustache like a comic villain. "Oh yes, it's because I have life experience, and I'm incredibly insightful, despite what my wife says."

"I'm not saying I'm in love with Rae." He wasn't ready for full transparency yet. He couldn't have his friends and family thinking he was some sort of loser who loved women who didn't love him back, but he did think he could be partially honest with his brother-in-law. "She's interested in some guy. She's calling him a possibility, and I don't like it." He looked at the deflated punching bag in his hands. "I hate it."

"So, let me get this straight." Charlie pulled the backpack off his shoulders and set it on a nearby weight bench. "You don't want to have a relationship with Rae, but you don't want anyone else to either?"

Man, when he put it that way it made him sound like a scumbag. Was that really what he was doing?

"I mean, yeah?" Gabriel sighed and sat on the weight bench next to Charlie's backpack. "That's bad, isn't it?"

"It's not good." He told him honestly. "You've got to either date her or let her go. It's not fair to her to hold her back, man."

He was right. Charlie was one hundred percent, completely right. It was unfair to Rae for him to treat her as if he intended their relationship to become more, when he had no such intentions. He needed to let her go.

And he needed to move on himself. At that moment he remembered that Charlie and Camila had met through an online dating site.

Charlie had unzipped his backpack and pulled out his headphones and was putting them on, preparing for a strenuous workout, no doubt.

"Hey, I set up an online dating profile."

Charlie's eyebrows went up.

"Could you help me decide who to go out with? I've never done this before, and I don't want a – "

"You don't want a crazy person." Charlie finished his sentence correctly. "Sure, I did online dating for years, so I definitely figured out how to weed out the crazies. We can look at it tonight."

They made plans to talk later, and Gabriel decided his workout was over for the day. He didn't feel like breaking anymore of the community center's equipment. As he drove through his hometown to his duplex, he thought about his dad. He loved his dad and missed him terribly, but his dad would've told him he was making too much of this. His dad would've said that it was cut and dried. Either he wanted to be with Rae or he didn't. Make a decision, son, and then get on with what was really important – making money. You're the only son. The only one to carry on the family name and to take care of mom. Get it together and build up that savings account and equity.

Gabriel pulled into the cul-de-sac that cradled the three multi-family structures he owned. It looked like most of his tenants-slash-neighbors were home for the evening. Kids rode on bikes on the sidewalks and one family had pulled a grill and patio furniture out on their driveway and looked like they were having some sort of party. They waved to him and he waved back as he pulled into his garage and shut the door behind him.

Chapter Seven

Rae stifled a yawn and shifted in the pew. She focused her attention back to the open bible in her lap. Pastor Kevin had been doing expository sermons through the New Testament all year, and this month they were covering First and Second Corinthians. She'd learned so much about the bible this year and could tell she was growing in her faith like never before, but she had to admit that these line-by-line sermons could get a bit boring. Was that wrong to admit? She hoped God wouldn't be mad at her for getting bored in church.

"In this letter, Paul is rebuking the Christians in Corinth, reminding them that their quarrels and dissatisfaction come from focusing too much on the temporal things of life rather than the eternal. As he reminded them in chapter four," Pastor Kevin pushed his glasses up his nose and leaned closer to his bible and read, "So we fix our eyes not on what is seen, but on what is unseen, since what is seen is temporary, but what is unseen is eternal."

Their pastor in his standard cardigan sweater, khaki pants, and New Balance sneakers, looked up at the congregation. He'd been Rae's pastor her entire life, and she trusted his wise words now just as she had through every stage of her life.

"Paul is telling the Corinthians, and I want to tell you, that a life fixated on temporary things like money and possessions and status only leads to emptiness. We must focus on the eternal – our relationship with Jesus and others – those are the only things that last forever."

Next to her, Gabriel cleared his throat and crossed his legs. Rae knew what that sound and body language meant. He was closing himself off.

The pastor closed the message and gave an altar call, challenging people to come forward for prayer if they wanted to make a change and focus more on the eternal than the temporary. Only a handful of people responded.

The congregation stood and sang a chorus as the pastoral staff prayed with people. Next to her, Gabriel stuffed his hands in his pockets and mumbled the words to the song under his breath. She didn't know what was going on with him, but something had him rattled.

The song ended and the assistant pastor reminded them of the monthly potluck luncheon taking place immediately after service in the recreation hall before he prayed the dismissal prayer.

"I brought chicken spaghetti, and I put it in the church refrigerator before Sunday School, so I'm going to rush over there and heat it up real quick." Her mom explained and then patted her elbow before dashing out of the pew to toss her casserole in the church oven. Rae had kept it simple and brought homemade cookies for the potluck. She reached under her pew and grabbed her plastic container of cookies.

"What'd you bring?" Gabriel asked her with a smile and a nod to her Tupperware.

"Oatmeal Scotchies." She knew that would knife him in the heart. He always wanted her to bring brownies.

"Why do you have to do that to me? You know that I think any dessert other than chocolate is a waste of time." He whined.

"Gabriel Matthews, there are two hundred other people in this church. One of them will bring something chocolate that you can eat."

"You actually expect me to eat something cooked in a strange kitchen?"

She laughed at him as they walked together to the rec hall. He refused to eat anything at potlucks that was made by anyone other than his mother, Rae, her mother, or his sisters, since he got sick at an infamous Mexican-food-themed potluck dinner eight years ago. Someone had made sour cream enchiladas that had resulted in a dozen congregants throwing up and having diarrhea for three days after the event.

She noticed a brown paper bag hanging from his arm.

"Hey, what's that? Did you actually bring something to the potluck?"

He puffed his chest and opened the bag to show her. "I brought two dozen dinner rolls and a bag of salad."

Rae put a hand to her heart and pretended to have

palpitations. "Wonder of wonders. I think you're finally growing up. You're bringing your own contributions to the church potluck!"

Gabriel chuckled at her. She was feigning mockery, but there was an underlying core of truth. She loved him, but he needed to grow up. Maybe a bag of rolls and salad was a sign that there was hope that he would grow up, after all.

As they left the sanctuary, Rae noticed Joe and Paige Donnelly exiting the other set of double doors.

"Oh my goodness, Gabriel, look."

He looked and saw their long lost friend's parents also. He turned back to her with wide eyes.

"I can't believe it. We should say something to them."

Rae nodded in agreement. The Donnellys had not been back to Family Chapel since Chet's disappearance.

"Mr. and Mrs. Donnelly?" Gabriel called out as they walked toward them. "It's so good to see you here."

Joe and Paige Donnelly turned to face them. They had aged fifty years in the last twenty. Both of their eyes were nearly colorless, and Joe had lost all of his hair. Paige still had her beautiful curly hair, but it had turned totally gray.

"Gabriel," Joe greeted and stuck out his hand for a shake. "Good to see you. You too, Rae," he added and patted her awkwardly on the shoulder.

Rae didn't know what to say. It was very good to see them back in church, and she didn't want to say the wrong thing. Thankfully, with Gabriel around she usually didn't have to be the one who talked.

"Are you sticking around for the potluck?" He asked them. "There will be plenty of room at our table. We would love to catch up."

"Thank you for the invitation, and maybe one day we'll be able to do all of that again, but," he paused and put an arm around his wife, "just coming to service was a big step. I think that's all we can handle today."

That made perfect sense to Rae. She admired them for making the effort to come to church. She could not imagine how hard it must be for them to go on with life not knowing where your only child was.

"Of course. I'm so glad you both came." Gabriel told them.

"We will be back." Paige promised. "We've decided it's time to start living again, right Joe?"

"Exactly. We decided to stop letting the past steal years from us." He looked at his wife and gave her a secretive smile. "We've got many years ahead of us, so we've decided to get out of our pain and spend them loving each other and blessing others."

Gabriel told them how much he admired their attitude, and Rae thought the same. What strength it must take to jump back into life and decide to bless others after going through such a tragedy.

They started to walk away, and then Gabriel added, "You know, I think of him almost every day."

The Donnellys nodded in unison and exited the church. A lump had formed in Rae's throat. She thought of their old friend almost every day too.

Rae and Gabriel stood silently in the church lobby for a moment. Then, she had to ask.

"Do you really think of him almost every day?"

"I do."

"So do I."

He grabbed her hand and pulled it to his face and kissed her fingers. Her heart fluttered at the simple gesture.

"You know he loved you," Gabriel told her.

What? Chet? What was he talking about?

She furrowed her brows, unable to say the question aloud.

"He did. Chet had a huge crush on you all throughout school, and he never told you. I wonder how things would've turned out if he wouldn't have – "

This was news to Rae. Chet had always been her friend. She and Chet and Gabriel. The Three amigos. The Three Musketeers. The Three Stooges. Was it true that Chet had secretly loved her the whole time she had secretly loved Gabriel?

She didn't know how to respond, so she started walking toward the exit, and he joined her. They strode across the church parking lot to the separate building where the monthly church luncheon would be.

Charlie and Camila fell into step beside them. Baby Caroline was snuggled in a contraption wrapped around her dad's neck, sleeping soundly on his chest. They chatted about their lack of sleep and Camila's fear of returning to work the next day on no sleep. Charlie put an arm around his wife and told her that he'd take care of the baby the rest of the day and that night so she could take a nap and get a good night's sleep, and Camila thanked him.

Rae knew the baby was a blessing, but she couldn't imagine the stress they were under. Camila was surely dealing with hormonal issues on top of a lack of sleep and facing the reality of returning to her job tomorrow. Rae didn't know if she could ever juggle all of that. She'd made fun of Gabriel for having to grow up, but she realized that she herself had quite a way to go before she could ever "adult" the way Camila and Charlie did.

The Family Chapel Recreation Hall was abuzz with activity. Rae's mom and Evelyn and all of the other church mothers commandeered the kitchen, bumping hips between the too-tight countertops. The pastor's wife, Maureen, took charge of placing the various casserole pans, appetizer trays, steaming crockpots, and dessert platters on the serving tables and assigning the appropriate serving spoons, ladles, and spatulas beside each dish. Lois and Evelyn and Brisa helped dozens of other ladies make the drinks and set out the paper plates and cups and put plastic tablecloths on the tables while men and teenagers set up scads of tables and chairs. The monthly potluck was an all-hands-on-deck community event, and Rae knew it was a throwback, but she loved it.

Once everything was settled, an elder prayed over the meal, and the serving line was open. Rae and Gabriel lingered near the back of the room to let other people get in line first. As people walked by them, most everyone talked to Gabriel first and noticed Rae as an afterthought:

"Loved your last video. I had no idea that you could get a loan to cover closing costs! Oh, hey Rae. How've you been?"

"Gabriel! Let's get lunch sometime soon. I want to pick your brain on the best ski resorts. You always put together the best trips. Nice to see you, Rae."

"My man! Don't eat the enchiladas! Remember that? That was terrible! You were so sick! Hey Rae, remember when this guy got so sick from that church potluck?"

Once most everyone had served themselves, Gabriel and

Rae grabbed paper plates and went through the line. They both followed the etiquette that a church potluck wasn't the place to fill up your plates and served themselves sparingly. Gabriel made sure to stick to his family's dishes and Rae's mom, Lois's, food, and Rae took small samplings of a few different dishes. They found their crew and settled at the long table with them.

With the noises of conversations and kids laughing and metal chairs scraping the gym floor all around her, Rae focused inward, contemplating her role as Gabriel's shadow. For that's truly what she was, a shadow. What was a shadow, anyway? The dark shape that's produced on the other side of someone standing in the sun. By definition, Gabriel was the person in the sun, and she wouldn't even exist without him.

Suddenly the food in her mouth lost all taste. She spit it out into a napkin and looked around at the commotion and realized how easily she could slip away. She doubted anyone would realize that Gabriel's little shadow was gone.

"Everybody is coming to lunch at mom's next week, right?" Brisa asked-slash-demanded all of the family members at the table.

Everyone nodded or mumbled that they'd be there, and Beckham followed up his mother's question with one of his own:

"Hey guys, did you all know that grandma challenged Uncle Gabriel to find a date, so he's doing online dating?" The eleven-year-old announced to the table with a grin, obviously delighted to be the one to share such an important piece of juicy gossip.

"Are you really, Gabriel?" Brisa asked. "Good for you."

"Don't say that," Byron shushed his wife from his place by her side. "No man wants to hear, 'Good for you,' from his sister. It sounds condescending."

"I'm not being condescending. I mean it. I'm proud of you for getting out there, Gabriel. The world has changed and there's no shame in online dating."

Byron silently mouthed, 'Sorry,' to Gabriel.

"Are you really online dating?" His mom, Evelyn, asked. "So, I won't get the chance to fix you up, then?"

Gabriel told his mom that he was, and for a moment, Rae was thankful to not be in the spotlight. She was glad no one was talking about her dating life and the same challenge her mother had issued her. She supposed there were times that the spotlight wasn't all it was cracked up to be.

"Aaannnddd," Beckham wound up like an announcer to the table, "do you guys want to know what else?"

Oh no. What else did the kid know? She would have to start watching herself around Beckham.

The adults around the table looked at the eleven-year-old, and his chest puffed and blue eyes shone, obviously loving the attention.

"Rae's bringing a date to the lunch next Sunday, because Ms. Lois challenged her, just like Grandma challenged Uncle Gabriel, but, do you want to know what I think?" His round face was flushed. This was his moment, and he reveled in it. "I think that Grandma and Ms. Lois planned this whole challenge thing so that Uncle Gabriel and Rae would come to the lunch together, like on a date!"

He ended with a flourish and sat back in his chair, grinning like the Cheshire Cat, clearly hoping his words would cause chaos and calamity.

Everyone around the table swiveled their heads to look at Rae and Gabriel, and Rae felt heat rush to her face. Next to her, Gabriel laughed.

"Okay Beckham, trying to stir up some drama?" Then he calmly explained to their families, "Rae and I actually were challenged by our moms, and both of us are bringing dates. I'm trying out online dating, and Rae's met someone who is a possibility. So, sorry, kid. No drama here. Nice try."

He smiled at Rae and patted her hand that was resting on the table, as if to say that all was fine, everything was normal, no need to fuss or worry about a child's silly ideas.

They were simply friends, and that's all they would ever be.

She needed to leave. Fake an illness. Make up an excuse about work she had to do. Anything to get away from Gabriel. She was in love with her best friend, and he was clueless.

Thankfully, one of the twins spilled something, so while everyone's attention was diverted, she snuck away. She felt bad for leaving the clean-up to others, but it was all too much. She needed to get away from Gabriel and his family and get outside and put her hands in the dirt to get some perspective.

An hour later, she was in her backyard sawing boards with her circular saw to make a window box to hang under her kitchen window. On the drive home from the church, she had the idea to plant herbs in a window box, imagining herself on a beautiful day with the kitchen window open and smells of mint, lavender, rosemary, and thyme wafting through her house.

She measured and cut the boards of extra wood she had in her garden shed and then drilled them together. After assembling the box, she painted it the same shade of happy light blue as the shutters on the house from the extra paint also in the shed. She laid the box upside down in the grass to dry and then went to her outside water faucet to clean her paintbrush.

It felt good to get outside in the sunshine and get her hands dirty. She'd intentionally left her phone inside the house where she couldn't hear it if it rang, couldn't pick it up to text Gabriel the second she thought of something to text him about, and couldn't check his Instagram to see if he'd posted something.

After cleaning the paintbrush, she laid in the grass and looked up at the sky. A few fluffy white clouds decorated the perfect blue backdrop. She thought about what Beckham had said at the potluck about her mother and Evelyn playing matchmaker for her and Gabriel and realized that it was probably true. She sat up and crossed her legs and looked at her paint-stained hands. It wasn't working. She'd immersed herself in an outdoor project with the simple goal of getting her mind off of Gabriel and her ridiculously embarrassing crush on him, but it wasn't working.

Was this how Chet Donnelly had been in love with her for all those years? Had he tried to stop thinking about her the way she had with Gabriel? She never knew. He never said anything.

But she hadn't been guilty of saying nothing. She'd confessed her feelings to Gabriel when they were seniors in high school, and he had rejected her.

"Oh come on, Rae, you know we'll always just be friends."

That's what he had said to her. And that was that.

The window box was dry. She found her drill in the shed and attached it to the house, right under the kitchen window. She stepped back and admired her work. It was perfect. Exactly what she'd envisioned. Next week she would buy herbs to plant in it.

Why did she have to be the girl his mom wanted him to be

with? Why couldn't she be the sexy and exciting new girl that he discovered all on his own?

Ugh, even though she'd intentionally kept her hands busy, the despairing thoughts still found a way to wiggle into her brain. Enough. She didn't want to be the girl who mooned over Gabriel Matthews any more. She was an adult woman with a life.

She washed her hands and stowed the sneakers she designated as her 'work shoes' in the mud room and then went to the kitchen to get a drink. Her phone sat on the kitchen table, but she forced herself to walk past it, certain Gabriel had called at least once and texted at least three times. She would no longer be so available to him.

She found her favorite tumbler and filled it with ice and water and made a cozy nest for herself on the couch with a thin blanket and throw pillow and turned on Netflix on her television. Normally romantic comedies were her go-to, but not today. She'd had enough does-he-like-her, friends-to-lovers, subtext laden, angst-filled conversations. Her real life had become a romantic comedy, only hers was one of those terrible ones that ended unhappily, as if the writers didn't know the rules. No, today she needed a good old western flick.

The familiar John Wayne movie worked like a lullaby, and she was asleep in minutes. Her sleep was deep and dreamless, and she let herself embrace the rest without worrying about what time she should awake.

The sound of panicked knocking alternating with the repeated ringing of her doorbell awoke her three and a half hours later.

What in the world?

The sun had set during her nap. She sat up and felt dazed as she looked around her living room. What century was it?

"Rae? Are you home?" Knock, knock, knock, ring, ring. "I'm really starting to freak out. Where's your spare key?"

Gabriel asked through the front door with a terrified voice, followed by sounds of banging and scraping.

Rae sighed and tossed the blanket to the side. She'd have to get up and stop him before he broke one of her windchimes or messed up one of her porch plants.

"I'm here. Calm down." She shuffled to the front door and

switched on the porch light and opened the door.

He knelt on her front porch with her favorite potted plant in his hands.

"There you are!" He sat the plant down and jumped to his feet. "I thought you might have a spare key under the plant. How is it that we've never exchanged spare keys? I've been trying to call you for hours. Is everything okay?"

Despite her need to put some distance between them, she giggled. He was funny when he was frazzled.

"Everything's fine. I just took a little nap."

She crossed to the white swing that hung at the end of her porch and sat on it. It was a nice evening. A few of her neighbors were also outside on their front porches and porch lights glowed up and down the block.

"You just took a little nap," he repeated robotically.

The tips of his ears reddened to a crimson and he took a deep breath as if steadying himself after an ordeal.

Had he been that worried about her?

"Sorry I didn't check my phone. Were you trying to get in touch with me?" She asked innocently, even though she knew the answer.

He swung his head at her and looked at her as if to say, 'What a dumb question. Of course I was trying to get in touch with you.'

She patted the seat next to her. "Come and sit down on the swing. You need to chillax."

He snorted a laugh and crossed the wide porch to sit next to her. He was wearing a t-shirt with his real estate agency's logo on it and a pair of nylon athletic pants and Nikes. But, true to Gabriel-style, even though he was dressed down he looked clean and crisp and ready to meet a potential client or to show a house or to have his picture taken for the local newspaper. When Rae got home she changed into yoga pants and stretched out t-shirts and got her hands dirty without any desire to see anyone. They were so different. He lived for the spotlight, and she loved to be alone.

He touched the side of her face with a finger.

"You must've had a good nap. You've got sleep marks on your face."

Her face tingled where he'd touched it. It annoyed her that

he could make her feel that way with a single touch.

She pressed her lips together and nodded, telling herself not to touch her face where his finger had been.

"I slept for three hours, can you believe that?" She laughed at her laziness. She couldn't remember the last time she'd napped like that.

"You must've needed it. You work so hard that you make me feel . . ." He trailed off and didn't finish his sentence.

"What?" She had no idea where he was going with that.

He shrugged. "Oh, you knew my dad. The highest praise he could ever give anyone was that they worked hard and made money. He thought you were pretty incredible."

He ran a finger over the knuckles on her hand that was closest to him, sending a shiver down her spine. How could such small touches from him do that to her?

She'd loved his dad. Leo. He was always busy. Always had the phone to his ear. Always rushing off to work. But, he was also funny and kind. He was a big dreams kind of guy who wanted a better life for his children than he'd had.

"I know you miss him," she whispered.

Gabriel swallowed, the veins in his neck showing like cords. His slid his familiar blue-gray denim colored eyes to her and she thought about the time when they were working together on autobiographies in the seventh grade. The teacher had instructed them to describe themselves. Gabriel had written that he had brown hair and blue eyes, but Rae told him that he was wrong.

"How could I be wrong about my own eye color and hair color?" Thirteen-year-old Gabriel had asked her as they sat at the dining room table in her mother's kitchen.

"Your eyes aren't blue," Even as a middle-schooler she'd been a perfectionist and a stickler for details. "Your eyes are blue-gray, like a pair of faded jeans."

She'd been immediately embarrassed for saying that, terrified that he would realize how much she thought about his eye color.

Sitting here next to her on the porch swing, his familiar eyes seemed a bit sad. He must be really missing his dad.

"How did you get a possibility, Rae?" He asked, his

whisper low and husky.

A possibility? What did he mean?

He must've read her expression, because he added, "You said that you had someone who was a potential date, a possibility. I've been wracking my brain trying to think of who it might be and how you met him."

This was what he was so bothered by?

She blinked and opened her mouth to answer, but then snapped it shut. Why should she tell him? He'd had numerous girlfriends over the years, and she never demanded to know who they were or how he met them.

She lifted and lowered a single shoulder and answered, "Just a guy from work. We're going to dinner tomorrow night."

Something changed in Gabriel's face at this information. He was obviously disappointed that she had a date, but why? Was he upset that she hadn't told him? That he didn't know the guy? Or was he upset that she was dating someone other than him? Or –

Another possibility occurred to her that angered her.

Was he simply upset because she'd found a date and he hadn't?

He'd always been the popular one, the one who always had girlfriends and multiple offers for dates. Was he mad because the tables had turned?

"Yep," Rae stood and crossed her arms in front of herself and then announced, "He actually texted me earlier and asked if I'd like to go to The Monarch tomorrow."

Gabriel lifted his eyebrows. The Monarch was the most expensive restaurant in Oklahoma City.

"Wow, Mystery Man is a big spender. Clearly he's overcompensating in one area for something lacking in another."

Rae narrowed her eyes into slits and without looking at a watch or a clock declared, "Gee, it's getting kind of late. You'd better be getting home, don't you think?"

Chapter Eight

The most horrible Monday in the history of Mondays began with Gabriel locking his keys in his Jeep. After re-watching a YouTube video showing how to break into your car only using duct tape, it only took him fifteen minutes to get into his vehicle. But, the delay made him late for a closing, which aggravated his clients and his broker. Then, after spending the entire closing apologizing and attempting to soothe everyone's irritation, he discovered that his phone number had been incorrect on a Facebook ad that had been circulating for weeks.

After frantically changing the phone number on the ad and attempting damage control by reaching out to anyone who liked the ad with the correct phone number, he snapped his laptop shut and pressed his palms to his eyes and let out a groan. Then he looked at the time on his smartwatch. Ten-thirty. Plenty of time to hit a drive-through for some caffeinated therapy.

He grabbed his keys and jumped into his Jeep and headed to Brothers Coffee, his favorite. He didn't usually spend money on expensive coffee, but if he wanted to splurge on a cold brew or an Americano, then he did it at Brothers on Main Street which had been the Cool Springs pharmacy years ago.

He drove to the small town's downtown retail area, which really only consisted of a mile long stretch on Main Street where historic storefronts lined both sides of the street and strings of white lights hung from one side to the other like a canopy over the street. Except for Flips Pancake House, Main Street had been predominantly empty buildings until a few years ago, but now there was the coffee shop, the Pink Poppy Boutique, restaurants, and hair salons. There were still a few vacant commercial spaces, like the old bookstore next to the coffee shop and the old bank on one of the corners.

When he pulled his black Jeep into the drive-through lane next to the coffee shop, he noticed that the signage had changed. Now, instead of Brothers Coffee the sign next to the window read,

"Joe and Pages . . . Coffee and Books."

What in the world?

He pulled up to the window and it slid open, revealing Paige Donnelly wearing a smile that he hadn't seen in years on her face.

"Hi Gabriel," she greeted him in the most normal way, as if she hadn't been the neighborhood recluse for nearly twenty years.

"Mrs. Donnelly?"

"That's right. Now I'm your friendly neighborhood barista." She said with a nod, her gray curls bouncing above her shoulders.

"But, but, what?" He looked at the sign next to the window again. "Joe and Pages? Do you own the coffee shop?"

"Yep, and the bookstore next door. Can you believe it? We tore down the wall between the buildings, and now it's a place where people can get coffee and books, which is a pretty good combination, in our opinion."

Her bubbly demeanor caught him off guard. This must have been what her husband's secretive smile and talk of living again had been all about.

"Before Chet disappeared, Joe and I had dreamed of owning a coffee shop and bookstore one day. We both love books and coffee, and we've always laughed about the pun with our names, but after Chet, well, after that we couldn't dream again for a very long time." She shook her head and put the smile back on her face, as if to say enough talk of the past. "Now, what can I get for the town's most famous realtor?"

Gabriel ordered a cold brew, and while he waited on her, he pulled out his phone and opened Rae's Instagram, the only social media she had, hoping to find something that would indicate who her mystery man was. There was no one new in any of her posts, stories, or highlights. He combed through her list of followers, but didn't see anyone that could be her "possibility." He even searched through her tagged posts and photos, but nothing stood out.

Who was this guy who was taking her to dinner at The Monarch tonight?

The Monarch. He knew for a fact that you had to make a reservation to dine there. What if he –

The window slid open, and Paige presented him with a

perfect looking cold brew in a clear plastic cup with the Joe and Pages snazzy logo of a stack of books with a mug of coffee on top centered in a bright orange circle. It looked happy, like a new beginning.

He handed her his debit card, but she held up a hand.

"Nah, I won't take your money today."

He opened his mouth to object, but she stopped him with a raised finger.

"Now, now, you take that free coffee, Gabriel Matthews. You spent a lot of time climbing the tree in my front yard and sleeping on my back patio in a sleeping bag." Her voice deepened as she added, "And I know you and your family have prayed for me and mine, so no, you won't be paying for that coffee today."

He thanked her for the kind gesture. As he drove through the streets of his hometown and sipped his coffee, he admired the downtown area of Cool Springs – the eclectic businesses in the retro-fitted commercial area on Main Street and the historic homes near the center of town were beautiful. There were large mansions and ivy-covered cottages from the early 1900s, built not long after Oklahoma became a state in 1907. After a few blocks, he turned onto Boston Avenue, and drove South toward his office. He drove in front of Cool Springs Middle School, home of the Bulldogs, where he'd ruled as the coolest of the cool all those years ago. A large red and white banner had been hanging in front of the school since the fall congratulating the middle school Bulldog football team on winning the state championship title.

His office, Spillman and Kayson Realty Group, was in a converted 1940's home, down the block from the middle school and next door to Be Sweet bakery where his old classmate Brooklyn baked the best cakes and cupcakes in town. He'd worked for Greg Spillman and Hillary Kayson his entire career, and been their highest earner every year for the last five. Greg had been pushing him to get his broker's license. He hadn't come right out and said it, but Gabriel knew that if he got his license that Greg would leave the business with Hillary and join forces with him. Greg and Hillary hadn't gotten along in years, and Gabriel thought Greg was looking for a way out.

Gabriel pulled into the parking lot in front of the house-slash-realty office and killed the engine of his Jeep, but stayed in the driver's seat, sipping the strong, smooth coffee. He could be a broker. Managing a group of agents, promoting the business, overseeing the legalities – he'd be great at it. Maybe one day, but it didn't feel right yet.

A picture of Rae in her fancy green dress at The Monarch with an unknown, faceless guy interrupted thoughts of his career.

A couple of years ago there'd been a Chamber of Commerce gala that Greg and Hillary couldn't attend, so they asked him to go and represent the agency. He didn't have a date, so he'd asked Rae to go with him. She wore a deep green dress that shimmered when she walked, and he'd never forget how beautiful she looked that night. He could close his eyes now and still see her in that dress, only now she was wearing it with some random guy on a date at The Monarch.

The Monarch.

He picked up his phone and found the number of the restaurant and called.

"The Monarch fine dining experience. How may I help you?" A young girl answered, not realizing she was speaking with a complete psychopath.

"Hello? I just wanted to call and verify my reservation for tonight?" How had he stooped so low? "I had a reservation for two at seven. For Rae Spencer and . . ."

He trailed off, hoping the hostess on the other end of the line would fill in the blank.

"Rae Spencer? I don't seem to have that name here, sir."

Shoot. The guy had probably made the reservation in his name.

"Oh yes, sorry about that. I must've not given you her name."

"Yes sir." She paused. "So, what's your name, sir?"

He cleared his throat. "Um, John?"

"John, sir?"

He thought fast. "Actually, I made the reservation for my boss, Ms. Spencer and her date, but I accidentally gave you the wrong name of the man she's having dinner with tonight. Could you read through the list of names that have a reservation for two tonight, and maybe I can correct my mistake?"

It was a terrible lie. He held his breath, hoping she would

buy it.

"Um, well. I suppose I could do that. You're needing to correct his name?"

"Yes," he laughed nervously, "I've made a lot of mistakes as her assistant, and I wouldn't want them to go to dinner tonight and the hostess call the guy the wrong name."

"Well, I guess that would be confusing. They might not even get their table if the names are wrong. You said the reservation is for seven?"

He had no idea what time they were going to dinner. They could be going at six or eight or even nine. Ugh, why did he think this would work?

As he was about to tell her never mind, that he would figure something else out, she exclaimed loudly, "Oh! I know who you must be talking about."

"You do?"

"Yes, we have a huge reunion tonight, and so there are only a few other reservations for this evening, and only one has two people."

How could he have gotten so lucky?

"Really?" Gabriel ran a hand through his hair and felt a bead of sweat run down his neck. Was he really doing this? Spying on Rae? What would he even do with this information?

"Yes. The only reservation for two tonight is at seven for a Mr. Carter Stayton."

Carter Stayton. Seven o'clock. The Monarch.

For the rest of the day, as he went about his business showing houses, responding to phone calls and internet queries, posting a new YouTube video, he kept thinking:

Carter Stayton. Seven o'clock. The Monarch.

At his desk he had a lull between appointments, so he searched every social media platform searching for Carter Stayton. There were thirty-two Carter Staytons on Facebook, twenty-six on Instagram, and hundreds of variations of the name on Tik Tok. There were Carter Staytons in dozens of other states, but none in Oklahoma. He almost quit looking, telling himself that he'd gone off the deep end, when he saw a connection.

Garner and Fox Engineering.

There was a Carter Stayton from Savannah, Georgia who

hadn't posted anything to Facebook in three years except for thanking people for birthday wishes, and he worked as an environmental engineer for Garner and Fox Engineering.

And his profile picture was a distant, blurry picture of a band onstage, taken at a concert.

People who don't put pictures of themselves as their profile pictures were the worst people on the planet, Gabriel decided.

But he wouldn't be deterred. He was a regular Sherlock of Social Media, Joe Friday of Facebook, Inspector Clouseau of Instagram. Wait a minute. Was that a picture of Carter Stayton?

Gabriel's stomach sunk. Carter Stayton was an environmental engineer who looked like a combination of an Olympic athlete and a male model.

He shut his laptop and put his head on his desk. Rae had a date tonight with the perfect man. He needed to puke.

The smartwatch on his wrist vibrated, alerting him to a call. It was Brisa. He sighed and ran a hand over his face and told himself to get it together.

"Hey sis, what's going on?"

"Before you say no, all I'm asking for is a few minutes of your time."

"Sure."

"You never hear me out. This will only take – hang on, did you say sure? You didn't tell me you didn't have time or turn me down without even hearing what I had to say?"

He exhaled. Sometimes being the only male sibling was exhausting.

"Go ahead, Brisa. What do you want to say?"

"Well, I was going to try to pitch Sticker Cutie to you one last time. I'm only three sign-ups short of advancing to the Adorable Level, and on that level, I'll be earning a significantly bigger percentage, but," she paused as if debating with herself if she should let go of her corporate dreams, "but we can talk about that another time. Are you okay? You don't sound good."

He let out a short, sardonic laugh and then admitted, "Yeah, I'm not good, to be honest."

"Tell me what's going on."

He hesitated, so she added, "Come on, I'm your big sister. You can confide in me, and I'll try my best to give you good advice or I'll go slash someone's tires for you."

He laughed. Brisa had always been protective of her younger brother.

"No tire slashing is necessary, but I do think I may have missed my chance on something really great."

An image of Rae sitting on a porch swing with her hair a mess and sleep marks on her face, her profile backlit by a streetlight, illuminating the outline of her tiny nose and long eyelashes and thin lips, each feature so feminine and delicate came unbidden to his mind. He'd always treated her like something he could put in his back pocket and pull out when he was ready for it, like maybe when he was forty and it was time to settle down. What if he'd waited too long?

"A real estate investment?" His sister asked, just like a Matthews. Dad would've been proud.

"No, this is something personal."

"Hmm," Brisa intoned.

Gabriel expected her to guess like Charlie had, but she didn't. Instead, she applied classic Leo Matthews logic.

"If you know what you want now, then it's not too late. It's never too late. People try to impose all kinds of boundaries that aren't real. Don't take no for an answer, and work for what you want, Gabriel. Isn't that what dad always taught us?"

It was true. Dad had always taught them that if they worked hard they could achieve anything, but he didn't know if his dad's advice applied to this situation. He didn't want to get into it with Brisa, though, so he told her that she was right and agreed to listen once more to her sales pitch.

After turning her down again and her getting mad at him again, he returned to the office and tried to be productive. The agents took turns receiving walk-ins and call-ins, and this afternoon was his turn. He was fairly busy, and he was grateful. He didn't want to think about what he had planned for that evening.

After work, he drove home, pulled his Jeep into his garage, and thought about what he had to do. He needed a pep talk. This had all been Charlie's idea, so he called his brother-in-law.

"You really think I need to do this?"

"Absolutely, man." Charlie emphasized.

Gabriel groaned. "Can't I text them?"

"No, dude. You want to Facetime. They could be having someone else answer for them when they're texting. No, trust me, you want to Facetime."

Gabriel groaned again.

"Tell them at the beginning of the call that you only have a few minutes. That way you won't have to make up an excuse to get off the phone if you want to."

Charlie was full of online dating advice. He'd helped Gabriel select three women as potential dates, and he'd encouraged him to set up Facetime appointments one after another for that evening.

Gabriel went into his duplex and sat everything up. He popped a bag of microwave popcorn and got a can of soda out of the refrigerator. If he had to do this, might as well have some snacks. He sat his drink and popcorn on the table next to his recliner and then he sat up the phone tripod he sometimes used to make videos. He clipped his phone into the tripod and aimed it at his recliner. Then, he experimented with the lights to find the right amount of lighting – too little light and it would look like a ransom video from a terrorist organization and too much light would make it look like a news cast. He'd learned a few tricks and gathered some tools from doing his YouTube channel. In addition to the phone tripod, he also had a selfie ring light and a light reflector.

He positioned his armchair in front of his living room bookcase, hoping it made him look thoughtful and sophisticated. He pulled the tab on his Coke and took a drink. It was time for Facetime call number one.

He dialed the number on his phone that was in the tripod and then re-settled himself. As he waited for the woman to answer, he wanted to punch himself. This was ridiculous. Why was he going through all of this trouble? Why not just ask Rae if they could try to date and see how it went?

"Hello?" The image of a blonde woman wearing a sleeveless black turtleneck appeared on the phone screen. She tucked a strand of hair behind her ear when she saw him and remarked, "Oh, you look exactly like your profile picture. I'm so relieved."

Gabriel laughed. "You look like yours too. Your name is Myra, right? And you're a bookkeeper?"

"Yes, that's right. And you're Gabriel, the realtor?" After he nodded in response, she continued. "Well, how has your day been today? Sold any houses?"

"Not today. I mainly focused on marketing today. How was your day? Where do you work?"

"It was fine. I'm at DuPree funeral home on the west side of town." She looked up at something or someone behind her phone. "Just a minute, Rebecca. I'll be down right after this call."

"Everything okay? Do you need to go?"

"No, it's fine. I need to go take care of something in a few minutes, but we can talk until then." She smiled. Her smile was nice. It wasn't Rae's smile, but it was fine. "So, if we decide to go on a date, where would you take me? What's your idea of a perfect first date?"

She jumped right in. Gabriel cleared his throat. It was weird to talk about dating with a woman he'd never seen in person, but he could talk to anyone about anything.

"First, I would ask you what your favorite kind of food is?"

"Italian," she filled in the blank and brightened her smile.

"Ah, then I would take you to Primo's, of course, the best Italian food in town. After dinner we could take a walk around Will Rogers Gardens to get to know each other better." He put a hand over his heart in semi-mock seriousness. "I promise that I would be a perfect gentleman the entire – "

"Wait." She cut him off. "Are you that realtor who's on YouTube?"

He didn't know if that was a good thing or a bad thing, but he couldn't deny it, so he held up a hand a said he was guilty.

"Oh." She didn't look very impressed.

He was about to defend his social media marketing strategy, but she was talking to someone else again.

"Rebecca, tell them I'll be down in a minute." She changed her tone. "What? Why is the body not ready yet?"

Body?

She continued talk to someone else. "Tell them I'll be down in a second." Then she placed her hand over the camera so that all Gabriel saw was her palm, but he could hear her whisper, "I'm almost finished here. This guy is that realtor who has a YouTube channel. Can you believe it?"

Her tone suggested she was less than impressed by his marketing efforts, but he didn't care about that. All he could think about was her mention of a body. Did she mean a dead body?

She removed her hand and politely smiled at him through the phone camera.

"Myra, were you talking to someone about a dead body? Are you at work at the funeral home right now?"

She nodded, "Yes, well, I'm at work and," she paused and added with a bit of a sigh, "I'm at work and at home. I actually live here at the funeral home as well. The top floor apartment is part of my salary."

She lived in a funeral home? Where were the dead bodies?

"Listen, I can tell from your face that you're not too enthused about dating someone who works and lives in a funeral home, and – "

This time he cut her off. "I mean, it is kind of creepy, but I could – "

"To be honest, I can't see myself dating a man who does online vlogging, or whatever you call it. Sorry about that, but I've dated enough boys. I'm ready for an adult relationship, so this is going to be a 'no' for me."

He thanked her for her time and then she disconnected the call in what seemed like a rather aggressive manner. Gabriel sat back in his chair. Had he been rejected by his first attempt at online dating? By someone who lived in a funeral home?

He took a drink of Coke and ate some popcorn. He wanted to be done with this. Put up the tripod and the ring light and forget it. Tell his mom she won and she could fix him up with whomever she wanted. But then his phone lit up with a text. He stood to read the screen that was still lodged in the tripod stand. The text was from Rae.

Rae
Weird not hearing from you all day. Hope you're good.

Funny how just reading a text from her lifted his spirits. He typed back:

Gabriel
I'm good. It's been a rough Monday. Thanks for checking in.

He thought about their encounter on her porch last night and the low comment he'd made about her mystery man and knew he should apologize.

Gabriel
Hey, I'm sorry I said that last night about your date. I'm sure he's a good guy.

Bubbles appeared and then disappeared and then reappeared showing that she read his text and then read it again, like she was weighing his words and how she should respond. Finally, she answered.

Rae
It's okay. I'm not sure if he's a good guy or not, but we'll see. And, you don't let Monday push you around. You punch Monday in the face and remind them that you're Gabriel Matthews and no Monday's the boss of you.

He laughed. She could always do that – make him laugh when he felt down. He looked at the notes app on his phone to see the name of the next woman he was supposed to call tonight – Stephanie Perry. He dialed her number and settled back into his chair to Facetime her, hoping the second attempt would be better than the first.

She answered on the second ring and came into view. She looked a few years older than he was, but she was attractive. She had strawberry blonde hair piled on top of her head and wore a bright blue scarf knotted at her neck.

They chatted for a few minutes about Cool Springs, where he lived, and the nearby sister city, Maheeny, where she lived, and Gabriel couldn't shake the feeling that he knew her.

"So, you're a realtor? Do you enjoy that?" She asked.

For some reason he felt like answering, 'Yes ma'am,' but he just said, "Yes, and you're a teacher? At Maheeny?"

"Oh no, I teach right here in Cool Springs, at the middle

school. I've taught seventh grade math there for over twenty years."

Gabriel's stomach dropped. Oh no.

He straightened up in his chair. "Wait a minute? Miss Perry? I – I think you were my seventh-grade math teacher!"

She giggled and coyly touched the scarf knotted at her neck. "I was wondering when you'd recognize me, Gabriel."

He felt sick. Even though he was thirty-four years old, he couldn't be flirting with his seventh-grade teacher. Although, more accurately, she seemed to be flirting with him. That was somehow worse? He didn't know. He only knew that it was creepy – creepier than dating a woman who lived with dead bodies.

He ended the call as fast as he could and then went to the bathroom to splash some water on his face to get over the shock.

Should he keep doing this? He asked himself as he paced back and forth in his living room. He didn't know how much disappointment he could take in one night.

But then he thought about the extra-handsome Carter Stayton, Rae's possibility man, and how he and Rae would be at The Monarch tonight eating prime rib or filet mignon, and he was here in his sweats failing at internet dating. When did everything change? He remembered when he was The Legendary Gabriel Matthews and had girls crying over him, fighting each other over him, offering to do his homework for him. sending him secret admirer gifts, and telling him he could date them on the side when he had a girlfriend and they'd keep it quiet. Since when did he become the guy who couldn't find a date?

And since when did Rae become the girl who had good looking environmental engineers from out of state take her to the most expensive restaurant in the city?

He shook himself. This was stupid. Not his style. He had one more woman to Facetime tonight, and the third time's a charm, right? Right?

"You've got this, Matthews," He pumped himself up and slapped himself on the chest. "It's go time. Let's go. This is the one. Come on."

One last time he dialed the number and then settled back into the chair in front of the phone on the tripod. After the third ring, an attractive, age appropriate woman with brown hair and glasses came into view.

"Hello? Is this Denise?"

"Yes, and you must be Gabriel from 'Match Me.' Thank you for following through and calling in the evening. I know it must be inconvenient."

Inconvenient in the evening? That was weird.

"No trouble at all. What have you got going on tonight, Denise?"

"Our hot water heater went out last week and now the washing machine is leaking all over the laundry room floor."

He thought he was having a rough night.

"Sorry about that. I hate dealing with home repairs. Such a pain. Do you have someone coming out to fix it yet?"

She wrinkled her nose and gave him a funny look. "Not yet. That's why I'm talking to you. Are you available tomorrow?"

Was she asking him to come to her house and fix her plumbing?

"Oh no," she paused and looked around herself in panic. "There's water coming in my living room now. What in the world is happening in my house? Listen, could you possibly come tonight? I'll pay extra if I have to."

"Pay extra?" He stood and got closer to the phone, not believing what she was saying. "Denise – ma'am, I'm not a plumber. I'm sorry you're having such a difficult time, but I really don't know the first thing about plumbing."

Her eyes burned him through the phone. "Then why did you advertise? Now, I have to set up a call with someone else. This is ridiculous. Thanks for nothing!"

The screen went black. Gabriel blinked. What happened?

You just crashed and burned at online dating, that's what happened.

He'd had enough. He ripped his phone out of the tripod, grabbed his keys off of the kitchen countertop, stormed to the garage, and fired up his Jeep. He knew where he wanted to go, but he also knew it was irrational.

Regardless, he pressed the button on the remote to open the garage door and backed out of his driveway and drove to The Monarch.

Chapter Nine

Rae owned one pair of heels. The black four-inch strappy shoes stood at attention in the top of her closet, as if greeting her every time she got dressed asking if today might be the day she would wear them again. She'd only worn them once – to a fancy dinner Gabriel had invited her to last minute. She'd worn them with her best dress, a shimmery green sheath.

"Let's dust you babies off," she announced to her shoes as she pulled them out and slipped them on.

She observed her elevated appearance in her bathroom mirror. She had to admit that she looked good. The neckline of the royal blue blouson dress extended to the tips of her shoulders, revealing her collarbone, and the gathered waist accentuated her curves. She'd always admired her sister's dress, but couldn't help but feel like a charity case when Claire had given it to her.

"Come on, Rae, take it." Claire had said when she'd handed her the dress while Rae was helping her pack for her last year in grad school. "I've packed two other cocktail dresses, and I need to conserve space in my luggage. Besides, blue isn't really my color."

Rae shot her gorgeous baby sister a look. Claire looked stunning in every color.

"Seriously, take it. Maybe you'll need a dress for a spontaneous date with a stranger." Claire had winked at her when she'd said that, and now Rae was thankful for her younger sister's optimism.

She thought about her sister's hopeful words about a spontaneous date with a stranger. She knew this wasn't a real date with Carter Stayton, but she felt he was exactly what she'd told Gabriel, a possibility. She perfected her red lipstick as she plotted out the way a relationship with Carter could develop. There was the possibility that this dinner could lead to texting or phone conversations, flirting in the hallways at work, hanging out with friends, and then, after a respectable amount of time, then they would go on a real date.

Her phone on the bathroom counter vibrated with an incoming text.

Carter Stayton
Can I give you a ride to the restaurant?

Rae froze, holding her tube of red lipstick hanging in the air. If he gave her a ride, that definitely bumped the classification up and sped up the "respectable" amount of time. She swallowed and looked at the woman in the mirror whose hair was curled and who stood four inches taller than the Rae she knew. Could she be this other Rae? Could she be the Rae who wore high heels and dated new men and moved away from home to take a leadership role in the company? But what about the Rae who was always there for people?

An idea occurred to her. Why did it have to be an either/or decision? Maybe there was a way to be both?

As she held her phone re-reading Carter's text, it vibrated with an incoming call. Claire. Funny how her sister seemed to call at the exact moment she needed to talk to her.

"How did you know I needed to talk to you?" She answered with a question, no sense wasting time with a greeting.

"The bat signal over Chicago, of course." Claire told her seriously, and Rae imagined a light in the sky over her sister's student living apartment complex that flicked on the minute her sister needed her.

"I just hope it shines all the way over the Atlantic." Rae moaned. "What am I going to do when you move to London?"

"I can verify that the bat signal does shine in London," Claire assured her but then added, "Only it's a six-hour time difference, so these phone calls will probably be happening in the middle of the night for you."

Rae humphed and sat her phone on the counter and turned on the speaker so she could finish applying her lipstick.

"Besides, you know you're the one with the bat signal. When have I ever helped you? You're always the one with oodles of wisdom, telling me just what I need to hear, when I need to hear it." Her sister's voice echoed through the bathroom.

"Yeah, right," Rae said, even though she knew it was true.

"You know I'm right." Her sister called her out. "You've always been my rescuer." Claire paused a beat and then continued, "Wait a minute. Are you saying my sister, the totally capable, completely unflappable, Miss Rae Spencer actually needs my help?"

"Let's see . . . Gabriel still makes my stomach flip-flop, but he has no romantic interest in me whatsoever. I'm on my way to dinner with a new guy, and I thought it was just a friendly dinner, but now he's picking me up and I'm thinking maybe it's more of a date. There's a possibility of a job promotion in another state that I'm considering applying for, and out of nowhere I'm curling my hair and wearing heels, and I seem to be having some sort of identity crisis . . . I think that about covers it."

Claire laughed. "That sounds like my normal, only instead of fixing everyone's computers, I'm writing about happily-ever-afters, but have never experienced one myself."

Rae detected the note of sadness in her sister's voice. Claire had always been a romantic. It was what made her such a talented writer, but it was what also made her so disappointed when reality didn't measure up with her stories.

"Hey, don't give up on your happily ever after. Who knows, maybe you'll find the love of your life in London." Suddenly Rae imagined her sister with a posh and proper British man. "Ooo! What if you fall in love with a guy with an English accent! Talk about swoon-worthy!"

The sisters continued their relaxed banter while Rae finished getting ready. Claire moaned about her dissertation and the complexities of moving to another country, and Rae complained about her men troubles and work troubles. Neither had answers for the other, but it felt good to talk to each other about everything.

Both promised to pray for the other, and just before they said goodbye, Claire added, "Have a good time on your kind-of date tonight, but don't have too much fun, because I'm still holding out hope that you and Gabriel are going to end up together."

After hanging up, Rae looked at herself in the mirror. Curled hair, perfect make-up, stylish dress – she looked like a woman ready for an actual date. She thought about her sister's last comment about holding out hope. Just how long was supposed to hold out hope? And, at what point did it become ridiculous to keep hoping?

    She picked up her phone and texted Carter that he could pick her up and gave him her address and took one last look at herself in the mirror. She wasn't sure about Carter Stayton, but she was sure about one thing: it was time for a change.

Chapter Ten

After flirting with the hostess, Gabriel found out they were seated at a table for two behind the bar. The back of the bar was lined with spiky plants in a huge mahogany planter, the perfect camouflage. Thankfully, he didn't need reservations for the bar, so he asked the bartender for a cup of coffee and a steak and spied on Rae and Mr. Possibility.

It was obvious that she felt awkward. She always touched her face excessively when she felt uncomfortable, and she kept scratching her chin and drumming her fingers on her cheek. He had to admit that she looked beautiful. Her hair hung in curls to her shoulders, and she was wearing a new dress he'd never seen her in. The blue fabric of the dress stopped at the top of her shoulders, showing her collarbone. He'd never thought much about a woman's collarbone until at that moment.

As for Carter Stayton, he was annoyingly handsome, but he didn't seem to really have his act together. The guy barely talked. It looked like Rae was having to make most of the conversation. Gabriel let out a sigh of relief. From the looks of things, they weren't falling in love.

The bartender delivered his steak, and Gabriel thanked him and began eating. It was fantastic. After he was halfway through the steak, he heard something coming from the other side of the spiky plants. Rae's laugh.

It was one of his favorite laughs of hers, more like a giggle. It was light and bubbly, how she laughed when she was carefree and happy. It was how she'd laughed at her favorite romantic comedy that she'd made him watch with her. It was how she'd laughed when they were sitting next to each other in class, and he'd shown her a caricature he'd drawn of the teacher.

And now Carter Stayton was making her laugh.

He peered through the plants. She was touching his arm as she laughed. He was smiling and looked pleased with himself. Of course, he was pleased with himself – he'd just made the best girl in the world giggle.

Gabriel couldn't eat anymore. He asked the bartender for the check and paid for his meal. He had to get out of there. He couldn't believe he'd done this. He needed to get out of there before Rae saw him and definitely before he had to see anymore of her laughing and flirting.

On the way out of the restaurant he went to the restroom. He looked at himself in the mirror while he was washing his hands. Still had the good hair and the gray-ish eyes that women loved. A couple of small lines at the corners of his eyes and a few gray hairs, but no potbelly and absolutely no dad bod. But alone. Rae had moved on.

Behind him, the door opened, and Carter Stayton stepped in.

He averted his eyes to avoid eye contact.

Gabriel dried his hands and stalled by patting his hair into place. Next to him, Carter Stayton thoroughly washed his hands, and Gabriel groaned inwardly. Was this guy washing his hands before he ate? Was he trying to win some sort of hygiene award? Gabriel wanted to say something, but what? Get away from my girl? But she wasn't his girl, and he didn't have any right to say anything.

Rae's date went to the hand dryer, and Gabriel cleared his throat to get the guy's attention. Carter Stayton's eyebrows rose and he turned expectantly toward Gabriel.

Now he had to say something.

"Nice tie," Gabriel muttered the lame compliment, feeling even more like a loser by pointing out that the guy was wearing a blazer and tie and he was wearing a Spillman and Kayson Realtors windbreaker. He was wearing a windbreaker in the town's fanciest restaurant. Classy.

"Thanks." Mr. Possibility replied, probably hoping to get away from him as quickly as possible. Men don't compliment each other in the restroom.

"So, ah, I noticed you're here with Rae Spencer. Nice girl. Are you on a date with her?"

Gabriel decided to just come out with it.

"Yes, I am. Are you a friend of hers?"

Am I a friend of hers. Am I a friend of hers? I'm her best

friend. Who are you, Mr. Johnny Come Lately?

"Oh, kind of. We knew each other in high school." Gabriel played it cool, smoothing down his hair and then his windbreaker, as if he wasn't really interested in this conversation and had somewhere much more important to be. "She had a big crush on me. I actually felt sorry for her. Good to see she's doing well, though."

He knew what he was doing, and he hated himself for painting his best friend to be some sort of love-crazed stalker, but he justified it to himself. He was only righting a wrong. Rae should be with him and not this stranger.

Carter Stayton raised an eyebrow and tilted his head. "She had a crush on you in high school? That was a long time ago, wasn't it? She's pretty successful now. I don't think she's losing any sleep over an old high school crush."

Gabriel could feel his blood pressure rising, but he wouldn't give this guy the satisfaction of knowing he was getting to him, so he coolly slid his hands into his pockets and responded, "Once she confessed that we were soulmates and cried when I didn't agree." He smirked in a way he knew was effective at making people feel uncomfortable and challenged. "I have a feeling she's lost quite a bit of sleep over me, dude."

Carter Stayton swallowed and took a step backward, as if conceding defeat. Gabriel had won, but he didn't feel victorious.

"Excuse me," Gabriel mumbled and left the restroom and then the restaurant as fast as he could. What had he done?

He got into his Jeep and drove. He didn't know where he was going. He just drove to get away from himself and what he'd said. It had been a terrible, terrible day, but he'd had no right to say that about Rae to her date.

He drove the streets of the little city that had been his hometown his entire life and hated himself. She had always been a loyal friend, and he'd told the story of her most humiliating moment to a guy she hoped to have a relationship with. He had broken every unspoken rule of friendship and didn't deserve to have her in his life.

He pulled into a random parking lot, not really even aware of where he was, and cried.

Chapter Eleven

Rae took a sip of water and straightened the skirt of her dress while she waited for Carter to return to the table. The date had been nice thus far. He'd been unsure of what to order, so he told the waiter that he'd have the same after she'd ordered, and he didn't attempt to steer conversation topics to be about him, nor did he need praise and affirmation from her every five seconds, like someone else she knew.

With his blazer and tie and good looks and grown-up career and kind manner, Carter Stayton was absolutely perfect.

So why did she keep comparing him to Gabriel?

He slid into his seat next to her without a word.

"Have you tried the asparagus, yet?" She gestured to his plate with her fork. "I love it, but I like it cooked to a crisp like this, and you might not."

He took a bite and then nodded in response that it was good. They sat and ate in silence for a few moments, and Rae could feel that there had been a shift between them since he'd returned to the table. But she didn't feel the urge to fill the empty space between them with her words. Either this date worked, or it didn't. No skin off her nose either way. She'd spent too many years putting everything into a man's opinion of her.

Finally, he spoke.

"You're from here, right? Went to school at Cool Springs?" He asked her.

"Yes, I left for a few years and went to college in Texas, but I came back."

He chewed his chicken piccata thoughtfully and then asked, "Do you still keep in contact with people you went to high school with?"

She wasn't sure where he was going with this. Maybe he was simply trying to keep conversation moving.

She nodded. "Yes, a few of my old friends are still around. What about you? Are you someone who keeps up with old friends?"

He didn't respond to her question. Instead, he set his fork down next to his plate and leaned toward her. She could see the beginnings of blonde stubble growing on his chin.

"Listen, I like you, Rae, and more than that, I respect you as a colleague. You're an excellent IT specialist. Our Savannah office could really use your talent. In fact, our IT director is retiring in a few months, and I'd like to recommend you for his position." He looked down at his napkin and touched his fork as if working up the courage to say something. "But if there's someone here holding you back from leaving, some high school crush you're losing sleep over, well, I don't want to waste anyone's time."

Hold on. Losing sleep over a high school crush? Waste anyone's time? His time or the company's time? And what had happened in that bathroom?

She looked toward the men's room door and suddenly she knew. That little weasel.

"Carter," she paused and wiped her mouth with the white linen napkin. "Did you speak to someone in the restroom?"

He looked around, as if nervous someone could hear him, and then answered, "Yeah, there was this guy in there. Honestly, he unnerved me. It was almost as if he was challenging me. I was afraid he was going to hit me."

Rae tried not to laugh. Carter Stayton may have had broad shoulders, but he wasn't the kind of guy to get into a rumble in the men's room.

She put a hand on his forearm to let him know it was all right.

"Was he about five-ten with brown hair and gray eyes and a huge ego?"

He nodded. "Sounds like him. Is he some sort of jealous ex-boyfriend?"

She wished she could say that he was some weirdo who used to be in her life and not her best friend who she had unexpressed feelings for. She was confused though. Had Gabriel confronted Carter to get rid of him? Why would he do that?

But the moment she asked herself the question, she knew the answer. He wanted Rae all to himself. Only, he didn't want her. He wanted to date other women and keep her locked away in an ivory tower where other men couldn't get to her, and where she would spend her days dreaming about him and presiding as president of the Gabriel Matthews Fan Club.

"So, what did he say?"

"He said that you used to have a crush on him, and that you'd lost sleep over him. And," he paused and hesitated.

Rae knew he had hesitated to avoid hurting her feelings.

"Go ahead and say it. I can take it. I'm not going to let anything he says hurt me anymore."

Carter reached across the table and put a hand over hers. "He said that you told him he was your soulmate and cried when he didn't agree."

Heat crept up the back of her neck as embarrassment and anger flamed up within her.

"He said that?"

The conversation had taken place at Chance Gilmore's house their senior year. It was one of those fluke days in January when the sun came out and the snow and ice melted away, and it felt like Spring. Everyone knew it would only last a day and the next snowfall or ice storm or downright frigid weather would return, so they had to make the most of it. Chance Gilmore lived in a large house on an acreage with parents who let them build bonfires and hang out, so that's where over half of the senior class wound up that night. Gabriel and Rae and Chet had been roasting marshmallows together when she'd said the most vulnerable, idiotic sentence of her life, and Chet acted as if he hadn't heard her, and Gabriel brushed her off. Her two best friends had acted as if she was an idiot.

And the next day Chet Donnelly had disappeared. Maybe he hadn't been kidnapped and had ran away instead. Had he left because she had confessed her feelings to Gabriel? She'd had no idea how he felt about her until Gabriel told her a few days ago. Had she made Chet feel the way Gabriel had made her feel?

She tried to fan away the guilt by changing the subject. She wanted to think about the future, her future, and stop looking backward at the painful past.

She asked Carter about the position in Savannah and he gave her all of the details. The Director of Information Technologies for the second-largest office in their nationwide company. An office on the top floor. A bigger salary. Professional respect. She'd have to move away from Cool Springs and her lovely little house and her mom, but she'd also be moving away from Gabriel Matthews and her role as his hopelessly smitten friend whom he kept around only to boost his ego.

Suddenly the idea of moving away seemed like the most logical and sensible choice she'd made in a long, long time.

Chapter Twelve

Gabriel lifted his head from his steering wheel and wiped the tears from his face. The bright green and orange neon sign of the Fresh Market grocery store glowed in front of him. Apparently, he'd picked the grocery store parking lot as the place to have his emotional breakdown.

He shook himself. This was ridiculous. You can't sit in a parking lot and cry like some sort of loser. He put a hand on the gearshift to put it in reverse and get out of there, but then stopped and looked at the Fresh Market sign again.

Ice cream.

For his entire life, if he ever had a bad day, his dad always brought home ice cream. He didn't know if his mom told his dad about his bad day or if his dad had some sort of Spidey Sense, but somehow, he knew. His work truck would pull into the driveway in front of the house, and dad would step out with a Fresh Market sack hanging from his arm, which Gabriel knew immediately was a gallon of his favorite ice cream – cookies and cream.

As he walked through the grocery store that was near empty after eight-thirty on a Monday night, he recognized the song playing over the intercom was one of his favorites from when he was a teenager. Did it mean you'd officially reached old man status when you actually liked grocery store music?

He found the freezers that held the ice cream at the back of the store and scanned the shelves for cookies and cream, but didn't see any.

Seriously? Could this day get any worse?

He settled for chocolate chip cookie dough flavored ice cream and headed for the self-check registers instead of the ones manned by an actual person. He'd had enough of people for the day.

As he walked down the cereal aisle, he passed Dustin Henderson who was teaching three employees something that involved an I-pad and some sort of handheld scanner. Dustin didn't see him, and Gabriel remembered what Rae had said about her mom wanting to fix her up with him.

What was it about Dustin Henderson that Lois liked so much that she felt made him worthy of her daughter? The fact that he held a steady job? That he could make small talk about produce? Or was it the fact that he'd never hurt her daughter? Dustin Henderson had never made her daughter cry, and Dustin Henderson had certainly never followed her daughter's date to a restroom and said humiliating things about her.

Something metal slammed into the back of both of Gabriel's ankles, and he immediately cried out.

"Oh my goodness! I am so sorry!" A woman's voice came from behind. "Did I hurt you?"

He turned around and put on his best local celebrity smile.

"No, not at all. It's fine." He told her and continued walking to the check-out line.

"Oh I feel terrible," she apologized and followed him.

"Really, it's okay." He smiled at her again as he swiped the gallon of ice cream across the scanner.

"Let me pay for your ice cream, or something." She held out a debit card for him to take, but he waved her away.

"No, it's not a big deal." He stuck his card in the machine and smiled at her again to let her know it was really okay. This time he noticed how attractive she was.

"Well, I am sorry. Have a good evening." Then she gestured to his purchase. "Enjoy your ice cream. Chocolate chip cookie dough is my favorite too."

Even though he didn't feel like turning on the charm, that's exactly what he did.

He raised his eyebrows and pretended to inspect the contents of her cart that had maliciously rammed his ankles and commented with a flirtatious tone, "I don't know what you've got going on in your basket. I never buy any of that stuff. Are you making a bomb or something?"

He'd betrayed his best friend and felt like a horrible dirtbag, but he couldn't help himself. An attractive woman had given him an opening. He had to flirt.

She giggled like he knew she would.

"No, I'm making homemade bread. I make a loaf every

week. It's much healthier than store-bought bread. You should try it sometime."

"Making it or eating it? Because I could definitely eat it, but I don't know about making it."

She laughed again, even though it definitely wasn't his best attempt at humor, and he looked at her while she laughed. She was about his age, seemingly normal, attractive in kind of a non-earth-moving way, and she wasn't wearing a wedding ring. He wondered if she had plans for lunch on Mother's Day.

Fifteen minutes later he was starting his Jeep back up, his ice cream partially melted, and a new phone number in his phone. She'd said her name a couple of times, but he couldn't quite understand her, and it felt awkward asking her to say it again, so he saved her number with the bread emoji instead of a name, telling himself that he'd figure it out.

When he got home he put the ice cream in the trash. His stomach was all knotted up and he couldn't eat anything.

Chapter Thirteen

Melody slipped into Rae's office while she was on the phone with Mr. Ellis. He was practically having a coronary over the never-ending hacking attempts. Melody sat in the guest chair across from Rae's desk and nibbled on a blueberry muffin while she waited for Rae to get off the phone.

"Sir, I think we need to make everyone who logs into our network use a two-step identity verification. We may get a little pushback at first, but the benefits are worth it. Besides, everyone will get used to it soon." She nodded as he agreed and then told her to go ahead and implement her idea. She finished up the call and then looked at her muffin-eating friend.

"So?" Melody asked between bites.

"So what?" Rae knew so what. She knew Melody wanted to know about her date with Carter Stayton, whom she thought was the world's most perfect guy and likely believed that Rae had been on a dream date with him.

Melody narrowed her eyes at her. "You know what I want to hear. What was it like to have dinner with a man who looks like that? Man, I'm not even dating him, and I want to send a thank you card to his parents for creating him."

Rae snorted.

"It was nice." She paused a beat. "The food was good."

Melody sat her muffin on Rae's desk and stared at her. "The food was good? It was nice? That's it?" She looked utterly disappointed.

Rae shrugged. "I mean, it was okay. He's a very nice man."

Melody smacked a hand on her friend's desk. "Let me guess. He's good looking, and he's nice, but he isn't Gabriel Matthews."

Rae grimaced. She didn't want that to be the truth, especially not after Gabriel's actions last night, but she still loved him and no one measured up to him. Logically, she knew she would have to make herself not love him anymore. He had proven that there could never be a healthy romantic future for them, but it was going to take a while for her heart to catch up with her head.

She didn't respond to Melody's comment about Gabriel.

"We're going to Martin Park this Friday to see the hot air balloon festival. Carter suggested we get coffee first and then go for a walk around the preserve as we watch the hot air balloons. Doesn't that sound" – she stopped herself from saying 'nice' again – "lovely?"

Melody picked up her muffin and took a bite before responding.

"Yes, yes it does sound lovely. It sounds a lot better than tagging along with him to a Chamber of Commerce gala as a last-minute date, or carrying all of his equipment somewhere to help him make a YouTube video, or going to an Open House with him to impress potential homebuyers."

"Are you finished?"

She shot up a finger. "Oh! I thought of another one. Or to his sister's house to babysit her kids or to his mother's house to listen to his other sister's mlm pitch."

Rae held up both hand in surrender. "Okay, okay. Point taken."

"Is it really?" Melody's face became uncharacteristically serious. "Because I think it's time you stopped living as Gabriel's Girl Friday and started living for yourself." She leaned forward, putting her elbows on her knees. "I'm sorry if that sounds harsh. It's just that I would hate to see you waste a great opportunity at happiness with someone else because you're so focused on waiting for Gabriel to realize he loves you."

She wasn't mad at Melody. How could she be? Her friend only wanted what was best for her. She told her as much and then promised that she would give Carter a fair shot. After Melody left, she closed her office door and pulled down the shade in the door's single rectangular window. She leaned back against the door and exhaled. Could she really do what she'd promised? Alone in her office, she closed her eyes and silently prayed.

God, I don't want to love him. Melody's right. He treats me like a personal assistant or a trusty old pair of shoes, but I do love him. I've loved him for years and dreamed of building a life with him, but have I misplaced my love, God? Please show me. If it's not your plan for me to be with Gabriel, will you please show me, and please help me to not love him anymore?

She finished praying and dried her tears and sat in her desk chair for a while in silence. She wanted to hear if God said anything back to her.

Her computer pinged signaling a new email in her inbox. She opened it. Carol from the third floor was having trouble with the printer again. She sighed. Better get to work.

She worked through the morning and straight through lunch, fixing problems for people and preparing for an afternoon meeting with Mr. Ellis, stopping only to go downstairs and get a latte from the coffee cart. The meeting with Mr. Ellis went well. He said they would implement all of her new ideas for hacking prevention.

After the meeting, she strode though the bright lobby on the executive floor with its modern art, plush furniture, and glass walls, entered the elevator, and caught a glimpse of herself in its mirrored back wall. The doors slid closed behind her, and she observed herself in the mirror.

She didn't exactly look like a successful executive. Her clothes weren't right, and she wasn't sure if her demeanor was right. Was she destined to always play a supporting role in her sensible flats and whatever-you-need-boss attitude? Sure, she'd killed it in her meeting with Ellis, but would anyone ever seriously consider her for the position of Director of IT at the Savannah office?

She turned from the mirror and pushed the button for her floor. Time to get back to reality and stop fantasizing about things that would likely never happen. She had a good job here. Mr. Ellis was retiring in five years, and she could take his place then. It made sense for her to stay here for her mother.

For Gabriel.

She closed her eyes and told herself to stop it. Stop thinking of a future with Gabriel when he wasn't thinking of a future with her.

Back in her office, she pulled a can of tuna and a sleeve of crackers out of her desk and had a late lunch. She finished her tasks for the day and opened the calendar on her computer to organize and prioritize her list of reminders and appointments for the next day. At the top of her list she saw two reminders for that evening that she'd forgotten about.

The commission meeting for the Phillips Project, and pickleball at the Community Center with Gabriel.

She sighed and picked up her phone. She didn't need to attend the commission meeting, but it was a very important meeting for Carter, so she typed out a good luck text to him. Then, she sat her phone on her desk and leaned back in her chair. She didn't want to play pickleball with Gabriel tonight.

Actually, that wasn't correct. Truthfully, she just wanted to see him, and it didn't matter what they did. That's why he could invite her to babysit his sister's kids or to his other sister's mlm pitch and she would be there. It didn't matter if he said embarrassing things about her to Carter. She still wanted to be with him.

But, she was trying to listen to her head and not her heart. She needed to be logical. He wasn't interested in a real relationship with her.

She picked up her phone and began to compose a text to Gabriel.

Rae
Since I'm just some annoying girl who had a crush on you, I'm sure you won't mind if I don't make it to pickleball tonight.

She shook her head. Can't send that. She deleted it and started again.

Rae
Hey! Sorry but I can't make pickleball tonight. You know, because I'll be home losing sleep and crying over you.

She told herself to stop it and simply send him a straightforward text. She deleted the text and began drafting another when a text from him appeared.

Gabriel
Sorry, Spence, but I can't make to pickleball tonight. Maybe we can go one day next week?

He was bailing on her. First, he tried to mess up her date, then she hadn't heard from him all day, and now he was canceling plans. It was becoming very clear that her Gabriel chasing days needed to end.

As she pondered a short and sweet reply, she received a text from Carter.

Carter
Thank you for the good luck wishes. I appreciate it. By the way, I think you should know that your potential is greater than you even realize. The Savannah office would be lucky to have you, but that won't be your final stop at Garner and Fox. You're one of the brightest rising stars in the entire company.

She sat back in her desk chair, stunned at Carter's high praise. Was it true? Could she one day be promoted past regional directorship?

She looked down at her phone again, this time looking at the list of received texts with Carter's at the top and Gabriel's directly under it. Her supposed best friend canceling on her and the new guy being incredibly supportive – shouldn't it be the other way around?

She texted thank you back to Carter, and then she texted Gabriel back.

Rae
No prob

She wanted to say more – What's going on with us? Did you really confront my date in a restroom? Why do you act like you care about me one day and then ghost me the next? But, of course, she couldn't say all of that, so she kept her response to two syllables.

Bubbles appeared. He was composing a text. She told herself to put the phone away and check it later, but she couldn't seem to put it down. Finally, a message appeared.

Gabriel
I actually have a date tonight. Can you believe it? Maybe my mom won't win her stupid challenge after all.

So, that was it. He had a date. He'd found someone. A lump formed in her throat, and a tear threatened to fall, but she swallowed it down and blinked it back. She wouldn't cry over him anymore.

Rae
Great! I guess online dating was successful, then.

Gabriel
No, online dating was a horrible failure. I met this woman at the grocery store.

Huh, you don't want to give your best friend a chance, but you're picking up random women at the grocery store. Terrific. Makes perfect sense. In response, she simply sent a thumbs-up emoji.

Gabriel
I have a hypothetical question for you.

She cocked a single eyebrow at the phone. This was so totally Gabriel. Of course his question wasn't hypothetical. He had a question relating to this new woman.

Gabriel
If you met a guy and had a conversation in which you told him your name repeatedly, and then made plans to go on a date with him, but the guy told you that he never caught your name, would you be offended by that?

Rae's head fell back against the headrest of her chair, and she let out a single-syllable bark of a laugh. *Oh, Gabriel. You are such a moron. Why do I love you so much?*
She didn't respond, but the texts kept coming from him.

Gabriel
She seems to be a nice person. She makes her own bread, like homemade bread. She was buying yeast. Do you know anyone who actually buys yeast? I couldn't understand what she said her name was,

because the music at the grocery store was kind of loud. By the way, when did Fresh Market start playing good music? And she sort of mumbles when she talks. So, I just put her number in my phone with the bread emoji as her contact name, and now I have a date with a woman whose name I don't know.

Rae shook her head at the way his brain worked and how he texted exactly what he was thinking, as he was thinking it. She texted back a suggestion that he should take her to a restaurant with a walk-up counter where they take your name with your order and then call out your name when your order is ready or maybe he could send her a link to his social media and ask her to follow him, and then he could see her name there.

He thanked her for the good ideas, and then promised her that they'd play pickleball next week. She told him it was no big deal, and she silently told herself that it was no big deal also. He had a date with another woman tonight, just as he had a thousand other times.

She closed out her workday by responding to a final email that had appeared in her inbox and then tidying her desk and office. As she walked to the stairwell, she was joined by a few co-workers who had also worked a bit late, the same half dozen people who worked past five every day. As Rae said her have-a-good-evenings and see-you-tomorrows, she realized that these were the ones who made their company great.

Speaking of greatness, Melody fell into step next to her as she began her descent.

"You're great, by the way." Rae didn't want to take people for granted any longer. Gabriel had done that to her far too long, and she didn't want to be guilty of the same.

Melody waved a hand in front of her face like a blushing Southern belle. "Why Miss Rae, I do declare you've flustered me."

Rae laughed. "You really are. You are an HR Wonder Woman. In my tenure at this company I've never had one complaint about your department. I've always received my paycheck and benefits on time, and they were always correct. New policies and safety trainings have always been clearly communicated." She threw an arm around Melody's shoulders and squeezed. "And thank you for being honest with me this morning about Gabriel. I need an honest friend. Except for the fact that you have an unhealthy obsession with live music, you're pretty perfect."

Melody straightened and held up a defensive hand. "Hey now, you'd better not be talking bad about my music. In fact, I'm on my way to a concert at LaFever's now. Want to join me? Come on, Rae, you need to cut loose a little."

Rae declined without giving an excuse. The truth was she planned to spend the evening praying and asking God for direction. She hoped the Lord would help her reconcile the differential between her head and her heart.

"How does that man look like that every day?"

Rae looked further down the stairwell toward where Melody nodded. Carter was with the late leavers jogging down the steps.

"It's like he's never had a bad hair day or a pimple. He's like an air-brushed human. How does it feel to be almost dating someone like that?"

Rae simply shrugged but thought about Melody's question as she exited the building and said goodbye to her truth-telling friend. She made her way to her car and saw Carter across the parking lot.

Melody's question came back to her: How did it feel to be almost dating someone like that?

Her answer was that she didn't feel anything.

He was in her field of vision, and she felt no compulsion to call out to him. She felt no quickened heartbeat or butterflies in her stomach or any of that stuff you're supposed to feel toward someone you're dating. She didn't feel like spending time with him or talking to him, but it was killing her that Gabriel had canceled their plans and she hadn't heard his voice all day.

When would she ever get over Gabriel Matthews?

Carter caught her looking at him and sent her a smile and a wave, and she smiled and waved back.

She got into her car and started the engine, found her sunglasses that were clipped on the visor and slid them up her nose. The sun was starting to set, and the sky was at its golden hour with hues of pink and orange streaking across the sky. It was a beautiful evening. She had a fun date with a handsome and kind man to look forward to this weekend. She could focus on the absence of feelings, or she could make the smart decision to forget about butterflies and fireworks and racing heartbeats. There was no rule that relationships had to have those things. The smart thing to do would be to forget all about Gabriel and fireworks and feelings, and Rae had always been the smart one.

Chapter Fourteen

"You want to use my glue gun to do what?" Gabriel's mom asked in unbelief.

He pulled a white glove and a bag of rhinestones out of the Wal-Mart sack he held. "To glue these jewels to this glove." He explained, somewhat embarrassed at how silly it sounded. "I'm doing a Michael Jackson impersonation."

His mother wordlessly looked heavenward and turned to walk through the living room to the spare bedroom where she kept her craft supplies in a closet. Even though she said nothing, he could hear her thoughts commenting on how immature and outlandish her son was.

He knew his videos confused his family, but they didn't see how it had increased his business. In the last few months his phone calls, emails, and walk-ins had grown exponentially.

His mom brought him her glue gun, and he went to work gluing the rhinestones on at her kitchen table, and she sat across from him with her cup of tea.

"You've found a date for Sunday, then? I don't get to bring a date for you?"

"Probably. She's very nice and attractive." He shrugged as he glued. "Who knows."

"She's from Cool Springs?"

"I think so. She was shopping at Fresh Market."

Evelyn pushed her bifocals up her nose and narrowed her eyes at her son. "What's her name? Do we know her family?"

Gabriel pretended not to hear. "How long do you think it'll take this to dry?"

She told him it would only take a few seconds, and followed up with another request for her name.

He grimaced, not wanting to tell his mom that he couldn't remember Bread Woman's name.

His mom set her tea cup down on its saucer with a slight clinking sound.

"Gabriel Matthews. Are you telling me that you can't remember her name?"

"Well, she mumbled. I couldn't understand her. I have a plan, though. I'm going to send her a link to follow me on social media, and then when she does I can see her name."

"Hmm." His mom intoned critically, obviously disappointed in him.

"What? I know she makes bread, so I saved her contact with the bread emoji. See?" He held up his phone and flashed his movie star smile.

His mom waved a hand at him and told him she didn't understand his generation with their Tik Tok and emojis, and he laughed at her, knowing she was half-pretending to be a grumpy old lady.

He went to his old bedroom to film the silly video that he planned to upload as a YouTube short that would drive people to his channel. His parents had repainted his old bedroom and redecorated it years ago. Now the room had plain white walls and a floral bedspread on the bed he'd slept in for years. His childhood trophies were no longer on the walls, and the closet and dresser no longer held all of his clothes. One thing that hadn't changed was his old bookcase, where his yearbooks stood in stacks on the bottom shelves and framed pictures posed in front of college textbooks and his favorite childhood books. There were group pictures of basketball teams, his prom photo with his date, Callie, whom he hadn't thought about in years, pictures of himself with friends at camps and goofing around, and of course there were pictures of Rae and Chet. There was a small square one of them in go-karts when they were about seven. There was one of them in a canoe together with other friends from the church youth group when they were fifteen. But then of course the newer pictures didn't have Chet in them. Pictures from his college graduation, pictures with his nieces and nephew – he and Rae together in all of them, like two-thirds of a trio.

One of the latest viral trends was to film yourself lip-synching to old classics. He felt a bit foolish pretending to sing the old Michael Jackson song and showing off his new bejeweled glove and moon-walking ability, but mere seconds after he posted it, his phone went bonkers with notifications. He'd officially gone viral again.

He sat on the corner of his old bed and watched the number of views grow. He'd never aspired to be social media famous, but oddly enough, that's what was happening. He knew this video would translate into more business. All of his professional and financial goals were on track, so why wasn't he happier?

A tap on the door interrupted his thoughts.

"Are you finished?"

"Yes, mom, come on in." He patted a space next to him on the bed. "Come watch it and tell me what you think."

He cued up the video and handed her the phone. She watched it and shook her head as she handed the phone back.

"I guess they're better than commercials. You don't have to pay for them, and they get more viewers, right?" She squinted her faded brown eyes behind her glasses like she was trying to understand.

Gabriel felt a heart tug for her. The last year had been awful for her. Her husband of forty-something years had passed and left her alone in this big, empty house. His sickness had been quick, which had been a blessing in some respects, but because it was so quick, his mom had been unprepared.

He put an arm around her waist and pulled her close to him. It bothered him that he felt her ribs. She'd always been a diminutive woman, but she felt too thin. Was she eating like she should?

"That's right, mom. Can't beat free advertising. I think dad would approve, don't you?"

"Eh," she paused and shrugged and nestled into his chest before continuing, "probably. He'd think your dances and pranks and such were downright silly, but the free advertising part he'd definitely approve of."

They both enjoyed the hug for a few seconds. His sisters had always complained that he was his mom's favorite, and their mom had never denied it. It felt good to hug her. He missed his dad fiercely, but he didn't know how he would handle his mom's death. He couldn't even think about that.

They released from their embrace, and both had tears in their eyes. His mom and dad had always been "Leo and Evelyn." You never said one name without the other. They were a matched set.

As he looked at his beautifully weathered mom sitting next to him on the bed, he was suddenly struck with a desire to call Rae and make everything right, to just come out with it and be honest with his feelings. He was certain his mom didn't regret the times she'd expressed her love for his dad, and she more than likely wished she had more time to tell him all over again.

"I will say this." She took a deep breath and patted his leg decisively. "You can't date a woman whose name you don't know."

He laughed. "Mom, it's not that big of a deal. I've got a way to figure out her name."

"At-ta-ta-ta," she put a finger on his lips to shush him. "If she is important enough to date, then she is important enough to remember her name. I don't want my son settling for some bread woman."

She swatted at the side of his leg as if to tell him the case was closed, and she got up and headed to the kitchen. Gabriel followed.

"Your son isn't settling for a bread woman. I'm just trying to beat my mom in a bet."

She laughed as she tossed her tea bag into the under-the-sink trashcan and then put her tea cup in the sink.

"Don't blame me for your poor decision making. I can't help it that you have a perfectly wonderful young woman that you are bound and determined to let slip away."

She pulled the dishwasher open in a huff and started unloaded dishes.

Hold on. She was talking about Rae. She'd never tried to fix them up before.

"Mom, are you talking about Rae?"

She was quiet for a few seconds but continued unloading the dishes. The clinking of glasses filled the otherwise silent kitchen as he waited on her response.

Finally, she answered.

"Yes. I am talking about Rae." She let out an exasperated sigh and stopped with the dishes and faced him. "I've held my tongue all these years, son. Your dad told me to keep my opinions about this to myself and to let you decide for yourself who you would date, but I can't hold my tongue any longer. Rae Spencer is an incredible young woman, and you would be lucky – that's right lucky – to have her."

Her face had gone bright red, and she fanned herself with her hand.

Gabriel blinked. How could he tell her that he already knew that but he'd missed his chance? How could he tell her that he'd treated Rae too badly over the years and that she had wisely quit waiting for him and had started dating Mr. Perfect?

She put her hands on his shoulders and looked squarely into his eyes.

"Please forget I said that. I don't want to tell you who to date. If you bring this bread woman to the Mother's Day lunch, then I will be very pleased to meet her."

"Thanks mom." He kissed her cheek and then patted her shoulder. "And I promise that I'll figure out her name before then."

"No worries if you don't, darling. I'll refer to her as Miss Biscuit."

Gabriel groaned.

"No good? How about Miss Scone? Miss Sourdough?"

He raised his arms in surrender to his mom's jokes, but she only continued.

"Miss Muffin? Miss Cinnamon Toast?"

After visiting with his mom, he left her house and drove home. Several people had already seen his latest video and had direct messaged him. Most of the messages were trash, but a couple were from valid potential customers. He planned to go home and follow up with them before his date.

He took a slight detour on the way to his duplex so that he could drive in front of Garner and Fox Engineering. The shiny six story building was the tallest one in town, and he felt pride at the fact that Rae did so well there. Her car sat in the lot across the street, like he knew it would. If it was a workday, then Rae would be there.

She'd always been that way. In school she'd received awards for perfect attendance year after year. His mouth twitched into a smile as he drove through Cool Springs thinking about her.

She'd always been so smart. They'd walked home from the

bus stop together all through elementary school, and every day she would show him the stickers she got on all of her A plus papers. She'd been a valuable member of the Cool Springs High School basketball team, not because she was athletically gifted, but because she understood what was happening on the court better than anyone, and she excelled at the fundamentals because of her self-discipline to practice her skills daily.

Gabriel turned into his neighborhood, and thought about himself as a high school basketball player. He'd been the polar opposite of Rae. Whereas she'd been the dependable sixth man who could always sub in when the starters fouled out or were playing poorly, he'd been the star who'd never practiced on his own.

Since he was a kid, basketball came naturally to him, just like everything else. Grades, friends, basketball – he excelled at all of it without effort.

He pulled into his garage, killed the engine of his Jeep, and sat in thought for a few minutes.

All those years Rae had practiced every night on the Matthews' driveway, because they had a basketball goal and the Spencers didn't. Many nights his dad would work with Rae on her free throws or her dribbling. Afterwards, he'd usually come inside and brag on 'that Spencer girl,' re-telling something funny she'd said or telling them how her skills had improved because of her discipline to practice. His dad had loved her too.

He pulled out his phone and checked his text messages. There was a message from the bread emoji that simply said, "Looking forward to tonight!"

His mom was right. If he didn't even care enough to remember this woman's name, did he really care enough to date her? And why date her when he had feelings for Rae?

He texted the bread woman back and kindly cancelled their date. He tried to be as honest as possibly without going into too much detail.

Gabriel
Hey, I'm sorry, but I won't be able to date you. Please don't take it personally. I have recently realized that I have feelings for my friend, so I have decided to take my chances and tell her how I feel. Someone

reminded me today that life is very short, and I should tell the people I love how I feel.

Chapter Fifteen

Rae's alarm sounded at six-thirty the next morning, and her first conscious thought was the bible verse she'd read the night before.

Proverbs 3:5, "Trust in the Lord with all your heart, and lean not on your own understanding."

The verse rolled around in her brain while she trudged out of bed and went to the bathroom and brushed her teeth. It echoed over and over in her mind as she made a pot of coffee, sprayed dry shampoo onto her roots, and brushed her hair.

Trust the Lord.

She poured herself a mug of coffee and took it to the living room where she looked out the windows at the morning activity on her block. Her neighbor across the street, who was wearing nothing but sweatpants, wheeled his trash can to the curb. His belly bounced as his bare feet padded down the driveway, and Rae sipped her coffee and pondered the proverb.

With all your heart.

She made her bed and told her phone to, "Play the news." The speakers she had expertly mounted throughout her house began playing her pre-programmed favorite morning news show, Rise and Shine OKC. Anchorwoman Hannah Orwell-Miller's crisp and chipper voice read the news while Rae applied mascara and slipped into the next professional outfit in her wardrobe rotation.

Lean not on your own understanding.

As she slid into her most comfortable pair of sensible pumps, she realized she'd been leaning a lot on her own understanding, on what made the most sense on her calendar and spreadsheets and lists. Sure, she'd been trusting in the Lord a bit, but with her whole heart?

She stopped in the laundry room on the way to the garage and sat on the bench next to her dryer and took a moment to pray.

Dear God, You know the struggle I'm in between my head and my heart. If it's not your will for me to have a romantic relationship with

Gabriel, please take these feelings away, and please open my eyes to recognize the plan you have for me.

She whispered, "Amen," and then made her way to her car to head out for another day of fixing printers, solving wi-fi complications, and battling hackers. As she drove through the familiar streets of her hometown, she contemplated asking God for a sign, but then she realized that asking for a sign might be another way of grasping for control, and control is the opposite of trust. She wanted to fully trust God, but she had to relinquish control to do that, and she really liked control. She'd even been accused of being a control freak once or twice.

She chuckled to herself as she stopped at a stoplight. She'd actually been accused of being a control freak more times than she could count, and by people who knew her best.

Yeah, the whole trust in the Lord thing had been a problem for her for a while.

She turned on the radio and tried to take her mind off of her inner debate. A fun pop song came on, and she cranked up the volume and sang along. She pulled into her regular parking space but waited to get out until the song was over. After she finished singing and bopping in her seat to the dance tune, a light knocking sounded on her driver's window.

Melody stood next to her window with a knowing smile.

"Music. It's soul therapy, isn't it?" Melody asked after Rae killed the engine and joined her.

"I'm not a music-nut like you, but yes, it can be quite therapeutic."

Melody linked an arm through Rae's as they walked into good ol' Garner and Fox.

"I have an idea," Melody announced as they climbed the stairs together. "Let's schedule music breaks throughout our day today."

"Music breaks? Are we in kindergarten?"

"No, but I bet it would actually increase our productivity. You know, endorphins and all that. I just so happen to know the head of human resources who might be able to make this happen."

Rae laughed at her funny friend and told her to have a great day as they both exited the stairwell at the second floor and headed to their offices. She switched on her office light and unpacked for the day. When she pulled out her phone, she noticed a text from Gabriel.

Gabriel
Sorry I've been a little MIA. I've been struggling with something, but now I think I know the answer. Can we meet tonight? There's something I need to tell you.

She wished the tiny hairs on the back of her neck would calm down already. And why did her stupid heart have to race and her face feel hot at the idea of meeting Gabriel? Her body betrayed her. All of her attempts to be logical flew right out the window with a single text.

She exhaled and told herself to wait a while to text him back. Don't be so available. Make him wonder if she would respond and meet him or not.

Who was she kidding? He knew that if he called she would always come running. That was their history.

She opened her desk drawer and put her phone in the far back corner of it and shut the drawer, telling herself to wait until lunch to respond.

Even though Thursdays were usually busy with everyone trying to finish their work so they could leave by noon on Friday, that morning the clock seemed to move in slow motion. At ten-thirty she decided that she'd waited long enough and pulled the phone out of the drawer.

She had twelve missed texts. One was from Melody. Two were from her mother.

Nine were from Gabriel.

Text #1
That sounded ominous. It's not bad. I want to tell you something good.

Text #2
At least, I think it's good – ha!

Text #3
Hope you're having a great morning.

Text #4
I just had the best coffee of my life.

Text #5
It was from Joe and Pages, as in Joe and Paige Donnelly. They opened a coffee shop and a bookstore on Main Street. Can you believe it? We should go there together sometime. Give them some business for old time's sake.

Text #6
Got a contract on a house! (Sent with a Gif of a dancing bear)

Text #7
Could you meet me at Joe and Pages on your lunch break?

Text #8
I was hoping we could talk.

Text #9
I wonder if you're not responding to me because you know what I did at The Monarch. Not my proudest moment. I wouldn't blame you if you never spoke to me again.

So, he figured out that Carter had probably told her about his confrontation in the men's room. Good. She hoped he felt like the idiot he was.

She threw the phone back into the drawer, slammed it shut, and let out an exasperated sigh.

"Ouch. Someone must've downloaded an email attachment."

She looked up to see Carter standing in her doorway.

"Something like that." She lied and then noticed the computer bag hanging from his arm. "Are you leaving early?"

"Yes, I'm rewarding myself with some time off. Since the Phillips meeting went so well, I've bought us more time, so we're not in such a rush. I'm taking off the rest of the day today. Some friends are driving in for a concert in town tonight."

"If anyone deserves the time off, it's you." She meant it. Carter had worked non-stop since he'd been there and had saved the company's hide with the whole Phillips ordeal.

"Before I go, I wanted to ask you again to consider the position in Savannah. One of my buddies who is meeting me at the concert is the head of the branch who'll be doing the hiring. I'd like to tell him about you."

After Gabriel's latest antics, moving six hours away sounded ideal. Her mother had Evelyn and the rest of the Matthews family and her church to look after her. Cool Springs could keep Gabriel as their town celebrity. She didn't want to be his fangirl any longer.

"I am interested." She sat up higher in her chair and looked Carter in the eye. "In fact, I'll email you my resume right now, and you can pass it along to him."

Carter smiled. "Will do. I think you'll be a great fit for our office. And then, we've got that, ah, that thing tomorrow at the park." He nodded again, awkwardly, and waved goodbye like he couldn't say the word, "date," and wasn't sure how to end the conversation and left.

Rae felt for him. How many times had she felt exactly the same way – unsure of what to say in social settings and awkward with interpersonal communication? She felt much more comfortable with computers than she did with people, and it seemed Carter felt more comfortable with numbers than he did people. They were a lot alike.

And Gabriel was their stark opposite. He knew what to say in every social context. People all over the world loved him.

It begged the question: should you be with someone like yourself, or someone who is your opposite?

She looked again at her open office door where Carter had been standing. She didn't feel overwhelmingly in love with him, but maybe overwhelming love was overrated. She pulled her phone out of her drawer and told Gabriel that she would meet him at Joe and Pages in fifteen minutes.

Her text brought an immediate celebratory response from Gabriel with balloons and confetti exploding on her phone screen, appropriate for the guy who was always a one-man party.

She got into her old car and drove the few blocks to downtown and thought about what building a life with Gabriel would look like. Gabriel as a life partner. Gabriel as a dad. If she married him, she definitely wouldn't be bored. There would be lots of laughter and craziness. She could see him suggesting unplanned, spontaneous vacations and themed birthday parties. Life as his best friend had always been so much fun, so she assumed life as his wife would be too.

She stopped at the light on Boston Avenue and her thoughts changed directions as she waited for the light to change. Of course, there was a downside to his personality as well. He was such an emotional person that sometimes he let those emotions get the better of him. She'd seen it as his friend. How much more would his future wife see it?

The light changed and she continued driving, passing in front of Gabriel's office and then Be Sweet Bakery and then Cool Springs Middle School.

All of this was mere conjecture, though. It was likely that Gabriel would never marry. The Life of the Party might never decide to settle down.

She turned onto Main Street and smiled at the familiar downtown area. She loved the old-fashioned storefronts that had been transformed into new businesses. She saw the new signage on the coffeeshop and bookstore and stared at it in disbelief. It was true. Joe and Paige Donnelly, who had been recluses for over fifteen years had opened a new business in which they would interact with the public on a daily basis? She shook her head at the strange turn of events as she pulled into a parking space on the other side of the street.

She jogged across the street, dodging the light traffic, and noticed Gabriel's Jeep parked in front of the business. His normally all-black Jeep had been wrapped in a giant sticker, no doubt purchased from Brisa. Giant pictures of Gabriel's face were on the sides and back of the car along with his phone number and website information and the tagline, "Trust Gabriel Matthews to help you buy or sell your home!" Gabriel's handsome smiling face in all its full color glory beamed from every angle of the vehicle. It was unnerving. The giant images of his head had to have been at least two feet wide.

She couldn't deny that she loved the giant face on the Jeep. She loved his wide gray eyes and his enormous happy smile that made everyone want to be around him. But she knew what the sticker on the Jeep meant. It meant that he would never leave Cool Springs. Ever. He would forever remain in this little town, permanently ensconced as homecoming king,

Years ago, she'd known that was the truth. When she'd decided to go to college in Texas, she'd partly made the late decision to get away from her hopeless crush, but somehow, she'd been drawn back to her mom, her hometown, and her gut-wrenching undeniable love for Gabriel. She'd decided back then that even if she couldn't be in a relationship with him that at least she could be in his orbit. But things had changed. It was no longer enough.

As she stepped onto the sidewalk she saw him through the large glass window. He was seated at a round table in the center of the coffeeshop, holding court. Three people were gathered around him, all fixated on him as he appeared to be telling a story. His animated face and gestures crescendoed to a flourish, and his audience laughed and clapped right on cue.

Their applause and laughter cemented the reality for Rae. Gabriel Matthews would never leave Cool Springs. If she took a job and moved to Georgia, it would be the end of any hope of a relationship between them.

Chapter Sixteen

He'd been telling Joe and Paige and the few daytime coffee drinkers at their coffeeshop about some of the funny comments he'd received on his YouTube channel. They got a laugh out of his stories, and it made him feel good to put a smile on Joe and Paige's faces.

The bell on the door of the coffeeshop jangled as the laughter died down.

"Rae!" He stood and crossed to her. He hadn't seen her in person since Sunday. Four days. He couldn't remember the last time they'd gone that long without seeing each other. He wanted to reach down and hug her and plant a kiss on her, but he stopped himself.

"I ordered an iced latte for you. I hope that's okay."

She didn't respond and joined him at his table.

When she didn't say anything, it made him nervous.

"I was an idiot."

She raised a single eyebrow in response.

"Okay, I *am* an idiot."

She pulled her chin down in a slight, curt nod.

"And I did something really stupid." He leaned across the table and touched her hand. "I've had a lot on my mind lately with my dad's death and –"

She pulled her hand away. Was she rejecting his apology?

He cleared his throat, wanting to do better, wanting to really apologize.

"I should not have gone to The Monarch that night. It was dumb."

She didn't respond. He should've known. She deserved more than an apology. She deserved the truth. She deserved to know how he really felt, once and for all.

"The truth is, Rae, I went to The Monarch because I felt threatened. I was afraid that someone was going to take –"

"Well, hello, Rae. It's so good to see you here." Paige

Donnelly slid Rae's drink in front of her and then patted her shoulder.

"Hi Mrs. Donnelly." Rae stood and hugged their neighbor. "Your coffee shop is great. I can't wait to check out the bookstore."

Paige laughed as she nodded toward the connecting bookstore. "Oh, that part is Joe's. He loves his books." Her face changed suddenly serious. "Listen, would it be okay if I talked to you two for a minute? There's something I feel that I need to tell you."

Rae welcomed her to their table telling her that they would love to chat with her, but Gabriel felt annoyed. He was going to confess his feelings to Rae. He wished he could say no to Paige Donnelly, but how could you say no to a woman who had lost her son?

"It's about Chet." She smoothed the apron she wore with both of her hands and looked up at them, tears in her eyes. "It's time to tell you both the truth."

The truth? Was she talking about his disappearance? Gabriel drew his eyebrows together and looked at Rae whose shoulder slightly, almost imperceptibly, moved up. In two minute gestures they had an entire conversation, both agreeing that they had no idea what Paige was going to tell them.

"We had been fighting terribly for months. He wanted to start a business, and we wanted him to go to college. He didn't want to go to church anymore, and we argued with him about that. His grades were slipping, but he didn't care. Looking back, I realize that all of those were differences that a lot of parents go through with their kids, but at the time it felt like we were the only ones going through it. Joe and I didn't open up to anyone about it, but the fights at home had gotten pretty bad between us and Chet."

Gabriel and Rae shared a look. Neither of them had known.

"When he disappeared, we had no idea what had happened to him. We couldn't imagine our son running away. He hadn't left a note. Even his best friends had no idea what happened to him."

She put a hand on Gabriel's arm and another on Rae's.

"He loved you both. That was one of the reasons why I insisted for nearly a year that he had to have been kidnapped. He wouldn't have run away without telling you two where he was going." She sniffled and pulled a tissue out of the pocket of her jeans and wiped her nose as she continued, "But the police and private investigator insisted that they believed he had run away. Then, eleven months after the disappearance, the private investigator found him. He gave us Chet's address in Arizona, and Joe and I drove fourteen hours to get our son and bring him back home."

She sat back in her chair, obviously needing to take a moment to collect herself.

Gabriel couldn't believe it. For seventeen years he thought Chet had been kidnapped or murdered, and not only had he believed that, but the entire town had believed it.

"Mrs. Donnelly," Rae asked, "are you saying that Chet is alive, and you know where he is?"

"Yes," she whispered, as if ashamed. "When we saw him in Phoenix, he wanted nothing to do with us. He was still so angry. We drove back home brokenhearted. Over the years, I've continued writing letters to him, and for years they were returned unopened. We lost contact with him for a while. When the letters came back stamped 'Wrong Address,' we knew he'd moved. We had the private investigator track him down again, only to repeat the whole argument and returned letters all over again. For years it was like that – us tracking him down, reaching out to him, and him rejecting us. But all of that changed three months ago."

She put on a smile that looked hopeful, but also wary, like someone who had been hurt so many times they weren't sure if they could fully trust good news.

"He called us. Well, he called Joe. We were praying together in our living room one evening when his cell phone rang. It was Chet. He told us that he'd moved to Fort Worth, and that he and his girlfriend are expecting a baby. He apologized and said he was ready to make things right with us. We have Facetimed him a couple of times, and we're driving down to Texas next weekend to have dinner with him." Her face beamed through tears. "We are going to have a grandbaby in a few weeks! Can you believe it?"

Gabriel and Rae celebrated with her. They all called Joe over to the table, and they celebrated with him too. They hugged both of them and Rae bubbled over with joy and tears along with Paige, and Gabriel clapped Joe on the back and called him grandpa.

After the celebration, and after the Donnellys returned to their work, Gabriel downed the rest of his coffee in a single gulp – for courage. It was time to tell Rae the truth about his feelings for her. He would no longer live a lie like Joe and Paige had for so many years.

"Rae, I need to tell you something."

She set her latte on the table and stopped him. "Let me tell you something first. The company has an open position in Savannah, and I'm considering applying." She paused and then added, "Actually, I already have applied."

She was considering moving? To another state?

The revelation continued to reverberate in his mind as she explained the opportunity. It would be a big promotion for her. She would make more money. More influence. More respect in the company. Might one day be even more.

Through all of her reasons why it would be good for her, all he could think was, *Rae is leaving me, and I never told her how I feel about her.*

He must have responded, but numbness overtook him and he felt like a zombie. He told her how proud he was of her and how she was going to run Garner and Fox one day. He faked a smile like he really meant it, but inside he was so angry with himself for not saying something sooner. He'd had every opportunity through the years, but he'd always made some excuse – wait until you're older, it'll ruin the friendship, and on and on. Now he realized that because of his silence he had lost her.

She told him that she had to get back to work, and paused as if giving him an opportunity to say what he had wanted to say, but once again, he didn't say it.

"Isn't that incredible about Chet?" Was all he could muster.

"Yeah, incredible."

"Weird to think that we were such close friends and he left without saying goodbye."

Rae went to the trash can near the door and tossed her cup in. Gabriel followed, and they both said goodbye to the Donnellys on their way out the door.

"Do you think he was mad at us too?" She asked him as they stood on the sidewalk in front of the coffeeshop. "Because of what you said the other day? About him having feelings for me? I never knew that. Maybe when I –"

She didn't finish her sentence, but he knew what she was referring to. Maybe when she confessed her feelings for him it had been the last straw for Chet? Had his flippant attitude toward Rae and his enormous ego contributed to their friend's decision to leave?

"Rae, please –" he paused. He wanted to say *please don't move away*, but he shouldn't hold her back if she really wanted to go. Then he had an idea. "Please watch my YouTube channel tonight. I'll be posting a new video that I want your thoughts on."

She sighed and closed her eyes and shook her head, as if annoyed. She probably thought he was going to post another dumb stunt. She didn't know he had something else in mind.

He walked across the street with her to her car. She opened the door and got inside her little car and started it up with him standing inside the open door.

"Got another date with Mr. Perfect anytime soon?" He had to ask.

She nodded.

Gabriel exhaled and looked at the dark clouds rolling across the large gray sky. It was May in Oklahoma, and that meant storms were always a possibility.

"Enjoy the rest of your day and kick rear and take names at good ol' Garner and Fox, Ms. Future CEO." He leaned into her car and gave her a "friends only" kiss on the forehead. There was so much more to say, but it wasn't the right time. Timing had always been their problem.

"See you later, Gabriel."

He stepped back so she could shut her door, and then he watched her drive away. He wanted so badly to tell her how he felt, but he'd waited so long that it had to be perfect. He crossed the street to his Jeep that now had his face plastered all over it and felt silly. What kind of grown man drives around with his picture on his car?

Chapter Seventeen

"Mom? Can I drop by your house for a few minutes? We need to talk."

Rae decided to take a long lunch and go to her mom's house to tell her about the job opportunity in Georgia. It didn't matter to her that she was thirty-four years old and by all definitions a responsible and mature adult. Before she could take a job and move away, she would need to get her mother's permission.

She drove through her hometown streets that she could navigate blindfolded – the same streets she'd ridden on in the backseat of her mom's car, the same streets she'd ridden bicycles on, the same streets she'd practiced driving on when she had her learner's permit, the same streets she'd driven on to church, school, friend's houses, shopping, and on and on for nearly her entire life. Everywhere she looked brought back memories, and Gabriel was present in ninety-nine percent of those memories.

It was time for a change.

She turned onto Redbud Circle and the twin brick houses at the end of the cul-de-sac came into view. The Matthews' house and the Spencers' house, both single story brick houses with large fenced back yards and beautiful flower beds, had stood side-by-side for decades at the end of the block. For years, when Rae would drive down this street, her heartbeat would quicken when she would see Gabriel's car parked in his parents' driveway.

Her mom was waiting for her on her front porch, seated in one of her patio chairs holding her little dog, Arlo, in her lap.

"Hey sweetie, everything okay? You never come see me in the middle of a work day."
She didn't wait for Rae to answer before adding, "Come sit with Arlo and me. I've got an iced tea for you."

Rae sat in the chair next to her mom and took a drink of the sweet tea she'd made for her. Normally she'd talk to her mom about her hostas and the hummingbirds swarming around her bird feeder, but she felt compelled to get right to the point.

She told her mom about the job opportunity and finished with, "What do you think? Would you be okay if I moved so far away?"

Her mom took a long drink of her tea and sat back in her chair and petted Arlo's back a few times before responding.

"Rae, Rae, my little caretaker, always worried about other people before considering what's best for yourself. Did your dad's death happening when it did make you that way? All through your teenage years you helped me so much. You babysat your little sister and did a lot of the chores and cooking. Goodness, I probably leaned on you a lot more than a parent probably should." She pushed her glasses up her nose as if to get a better look at her daughter. "Did I make you this way?"

Rae didn't know how to respond. Was her mom saying something was wrong with her? She was just trying to be a good daughter, checking to make sure her mother would be okay if she moved. Why was her mother acting like she had damaged her?

When Rae didn't answer, Lois answered her own question.

"Of course I did." She set her dog down on his dog bed that lay at her feet and picked up both of Rae's hands and held them in her own. "Honey, I am so sorry that I made you think you always had to take care of everyone else. I love that you are so supportive and caring. That makes me so proud. But, darling, at some point you really do need to consider what's best for yourself. Stop worrying about me, about Claire, about Gabriel. What do you want to do? What is right for Rae?"

*****

Carter walked past her open office door . . . again.

Rae chuckled at him. He clearly wanted to talk to her about something.

She finished her to-do list for the day and set about the research into an expense management platform. She'd been thinking the company's handling of corporate credit cards had become dangerous with their growth. She read through the particulars and made a simple-to-read, highlights-only presentation so she could pitch the idea of a budget and expense management program to her superiors next week.

"Are you getting out of here at noon, or are you going to work late and make the rest of us look bad?" Melody stood in her office doorway and asked with her hand on her hip.

"I'm getting out of here at noon. Carter and I are supposed to go to Martin Park this afternoon to watch the hot air balloon festival. Of course, he can't even call it a date or bring himself to come and talk to me about it, so I'm not holding out much hope that it's going to be a life-altering experience."

Melody shrugged. "Eh, maybe we don't always need life-altering dates. Sometimes we just need to get outside and look at pretty balloons."

Rae snorted. "Well, I can't argue with that."

"Also, there's something you need to know, Rae." She took a few steps into her office and leaned her folded arms against the back of one of the visitor chairs. "I know you don't realize this about yourself, but you are an intimidating person."

What in the world? Rae opened her mouth to refute her friend, but Melody continued.

"Now, hear me out, I'm not saying these men are correct in their behavior. They should be able to talk to a successful woman without tripping over their inferiority complexes, but alas, that isn't reality most of the time."

These men? Was she talking about Carter . . . and Gabriel?

Melody continued her lecture on the fragility of the male ego. "No, I am not suggesting you downplay your success or dial back your awesomeness. All I'm saying is to take it into consideration when men have difficulty expressing their emotions to you. You're kind of a girl-boss, and that can be challenging to a guy."

Rae laughed, but also wondered if there was something to what Melody said. "All right, I'll take it under advisement."

"And, also, if you decide not to date Carter Stayton, feel free to give him my number." She scrunched her nose and twirled her fingers in a cute wave and left the office.

Rae finished her work, packed up her laptop and called it a day. She didn't know when exactly they were supposed to meet at the park or if they were driving there together or any specifics about this alleged date that was supposed to be happening with Carter, so she went to his office to find out.

"How was the concert?" She asked from his open doorway.

He looked up from his work, eyebrows high in surprise at the interruption.

"Good. They were more on the heavy punk side of indie rock, so I'm pretty sure I damaged an eardrum, but sometimes I like rocking out to music that bursts my eardrums." He grinned.

She noticed that he talked pretty easily when the conversation was about music, and then she knew exactly what she was supposed to do. How could she not? It was so obvious.

She cleared her throat in preparation. It was a strange thing to say, *you should really be dating my friend*, but there was no alternative. She had a suspicion that Melody and Carter were perfect for each other.

"I'm not going to be able to make it to the park with you today."

She paused. He didn't look too disappointed.

"But I think you should go anyway."

Still sitting behind his desk, he furrowed his brows in confusion.

"With my friend Melody."

"With your friend?" The poor guy was lost.

"Yes. Her name is Melody, and she's the head of HR. I think she might love music more than you do, although, I don't know you that well so you might love music more, but the two of you will have a great time figuring it out." She pulled her phone out of the pocket of her blazer and shared Melody's contact with him. "I just sent you her number. On top of being a music lover, she's a lot of fun and really wise."

She started to go, but stopped to add one more thing.

"And, Carter, she would definitely like to see hot air balloons at the park today."

He leaned back in his chair and crossed his arms.

"Would this have anything to do with an old friend of yours?"

She thought about it. Did it have anything to do with Gabriel? She knew she loved Gabriel, but even if she didn't, she also knew that she and Carter weren't a match, and that he and Melody could be.

"Not really." She smiled and hoped he knew she had no

hard feelings toward him.

"Will you still consider the position in Savannah?"

She paused a moment and thought about what her mom had told her. It was time to start doing what was right for Rae.

"Absolutely."

That afternoon, she went home and enjoyed the most beautiful time in her backyard. The potential storms blew over, leaving behind a calm day with very little wind, which was rare, so she worked to her heart's content in the mild weather. She weeded her garden and put a fresh coat of white paint on her little wooden shed. The spring perennials in her flowerbeds were threatening a takeover, so she dug up the gorgeous pink daylilies and green and white variegated hostas and divided them and replanted half back in her main front flowerbed and half in a new bed she had started on the side of her house. She threw the blue and yellow pillows from her front porch swing into the washing machine and then the dryer, and fluffed them back out and re-positioned them onto the swing.

Then she made herself a pitcher of iced tea and cooked a frozen pizza and ate the entire thing as she sat on her swing and read a book. After the sun went down, she flipped on the porch lights and brought out a thin blanket and finished her book. Then she sat on her swing and took everything in – a neighbor playing with her dogs in her yard, another neighbor teaching his daughter how to ride her bike, an elderly couple on an evening stroll.

When she was ready to go to bed, she went inside and walked around her house as she brushed her teeth. Every room in her home was decorated and organized exactly as she wanted it. Her television was small, but her bookcases were full, and she had a million colorful throw pillows and rugs all over the place. Art that she liked hung on the walls. The toilet seat was never left up; no one ever put an empty carton of milk in the refrigerator; cabinet doors were always closed, and she never left the house with her bed unmade.

She even had a collection of state spoons she was proud of. Gabriel liked to poke fun at her about them, but she loved her spoons from every state.

She quite liked her little life.

She finished brushing her teeth and washed and

moisturized her face and then got into bed. She prayed before going to sleep, thanking God for her many blessings, for the peace and joy she had in her singleness, and then she slept straight through the night – a deep, restful sleep that can only be experienced by those who are at peace with God and with themselves.

On Saturday morning she awoke feeling better than she had in ages. She remembered that the next day would be Mother's Day, and she didn't have a date to the dinner. Her mother had won. Oh well.

She picked up her phone to tell her mom to go ahead and fix her up, presumably with Dustin Henderson, her mother's favorite eligible bachelor. But when she picked up her phone she noticed several missed texts and calls from Melody. In her texts, Melody begged her to call her, insisting that she needed to speak with her immediately. The texts sounded so urgent that Rae didn't even brush her teeth or go to the bathroom before calling her.

"Is everything okay?" She asked as soon as Melody answered.

"Girl. Your world turned upside down last night, and you don't even know! Have you seen Gabriel's latest video?"

Rae closed her eyes. YouTube? Is that all this was?

"No, I forgot about watching it last night."

Melody squealed, and Rae held the phone away from her ear. It was too early for squealing.

"The entire world is in love with you, Rae Spencer. I'm sending it to you right now. I know you don't really care about number of views or likes or comments, but this thing went viral in a matter of hours. It's already got nearly a million views. Who knows how big it's going to get! And, I also went out with Carter, but we'll talk about that later. Right now, you go watch that video!"

After promising to watch Gabriel's video, she put the phone down and went about her morning routine: bathroom, teeth brushing, vitamins, making a cup of coffee, bible reading, prayer. She was about to write out a grocery list when something stopped her.

Watch the video.

She sighed and obeyed. Her phone screen was lit up like a

Christmas tree with red circles indicating notifications on every possible communication platform. She had dozens of texts, direct messages on Instagram, voicemails, and even emails. She assumed Gabriel's video that Melody declared had "turned her world upside down" was the reason for all of the attention. She found Melody's text with the video link and opened it.

A close up of Gabriel's face came into view, and as he quietly spoke the text of his words typed across the screen.

"Have you ever fallen in love with your best friend?"

Oh my goodness.

"Listen, if you've got a real best friend, someone you have fun with, trust with all of your secrets, someone you can truly be yourself with, someone who gets you . . .then you have something so rare and so special that you need to hold on to that person for dear life, but, hear me out, but what if you fall in love with that person?"

As she watched the video, her mouth went dry. She couldn't believe he was saying this to the whole world, but the way he looked into the camera made her think he was saying it directly to her. She knew their relationship was rare and special, and she wanted to hold on to him for dear life as well. She just didn't know he felt the same way.

"Should you tell them and risk ruining the friendship? I've been struggling with this for a few years. Anyone who knows me knows that my best friend, ride or die, pickleball and babysitting partner is an amazing woman named Rae, and I am taking a risk. I want her and everyone else to know that I am in love with her.

You guys, she is so smart and pretty, and she doesn't need me at all. Like, seriously, she's perfectly fine on her own, but I'm the one who is an absolute wreck without her. She went on a date with someone else a few days ago, and I almost lost my mind.

So, I'm putting it out there. Rae Spencer, I love you, and I don't want to just be your friend anymore."

Chapter Eighteen

Gabriel didn't sleep at all that night. He made the video, pouring his heart out to Rae and to the world, but then he didn't know what to do. He hadn't really planned what he would do *after* uploading the video.

He'd spent a lot of time planning the video. He wrote out what he wanted to say and practiced it several times. He spent time making the language as clear and honest as possible. At first, he wrote about how special she was and how he was so grateful for her and didn't come right out and say he was in love with her, but he changed that, reasoning that if he was going to do this that he would go all out. Go big or go home.

After hours of tossing and turning, he got out of bed at three-thirty and went into his living room and stretched out in the recliner. He found a re-play of an old golf tournament, turned the volume super low, and hoped it would lull him to sleep, but after twenty minutes he gave up. He went to the kitchen and ate a spoonful of peanut butter and half a glass of milk and went back to the recliner, hoping that maybe something on his stomach would do the trick, but, nope.

He turned off the television and stood at his front door, looking out at the small development of duplexes he'd built. His dad had always been so proud of Gabriel's money-making ability. He missed his dad. Leo Matthews had been a great dad. He taught Gabriel to serve God, to take care of his family, to be a hard worker, and to prepare for the future.

Gabriel leaned his head against the cool glass window pane next to the front door and pondered about all his dad had passed on to him through his many lectures and conversations and realized that he'd never talked much about valuing people. He talked a lot about money. He talked a lot about building up your savings and diversifying and residual income, but never said anything about wealth derived from the people in your life.

Yet, even though he never said it, Gabriel knew his dad

must've believed it from his life. He remembered there were many times had his dad turned down opportunities to work on Sunday, because of his commitment to attend church. His dad was home for dinner every night, attended every game he ever played, took the family on numerous vacations, and treated his mom like a queen. Even though Leo Matthews never said that true riches came from the people in your life, his actions spoke it loud and clear.

He thought about Pastor Kevin's message from the week before. He'd said something along these lines, hadn't he?

Gabriel went to his room and found his leather-bound Bible on his nightstand and turned to the passage the pastor had referenced. He read the entire chapter several times and read verse eighteen aloud to himself.

"So, we fix our eyes not on what is seen, but on what is unseen, since what is seen is temporary, but what is unseen is eternal."

He closed the Bible and fell to his knees next to his bed. He'd had it all wrong for so many years. He'd lived for the spotlight and for the number in his savings account, but he'd taken God and the people he loved for granted. He'd treated Rae and his family and even the Lord like they were his subjects, his supporting cast, and his fan club. He asked God to forgive him for his messed-up priorities and self-centeredness. He promised God that he would no longer treat Him and the people he loved as if they were an afterthought. He told God that he wanted to change, regardless of Rae's response to the video. Even though he hoped Rae would see the video and say that she loved him too, he admitted to the Lord that he wanted to be a better man even if she rejected him.

His conversation with God lasted until sunrise. As light began to filter into his bedroom through the windows, he felt himself finally calm down enough that he might be able to finally sleep. He crawled into bed a little after six and slept for a couple of hours. He slept soundly and awoke feeling better about everything. Things between him and Rae might now work out, but if things between him and the Lord were good, then he knew everything else would work for his good.

He sat up in bed and reached for his laptop on the nightstand. He opened it up and clicked on the YouTube icon.

When he saw the number of views on the video, he fell back against the pillow and smacked his forehead with his open palm.

The video had more views than anything he'd ever posted. Almost a million people had seen him confess his love to his best friend. Now it was out in the world, had almost a million views, and he wondered if she'd seen it yet. It was nearly nine. She wasn't one to sleep late, even on Saturday, surely by now Melody had shown the video to her.

The comments and private messages were flooding in, and he couldn't keep up with them, so he texted his broker, Greg, and asked him to help him sift through them. He gave Greg his login information so he could wade through the responses and follow up on any that were real estate related. A lot of the messages were from women volunteering to take Rae's place if she said no, so he was thankful Greg would be handling it for him. Besides, Rae wouldn't leave a comment or send a private message over the app, and hers was the only response he cared about.

He checked his phone. No message from Rae.

Don't text her. She will see the video, and then she can respond how she wants to. You've prayed a lot about this. Trust that God will cause His perfect will to be done.

Viral video or no viral video, life still went on. It was a Saturday in the Spring, so he had open houses and showings scheduled for the day. He took a shower, drank a glass of orange juice and ate a granola bar, and dressed in a Spillman and Kayson collared shirt and chinos. As he headed out to the garage of his duplex to get into his decorated Jeep, his phone rang. It was Greg Spillman.

"Hey, I think you're going to be interested in one of these private messages that came in."

Gabriel wanted to tell him that if it wasn't someone interested in listing a house or Rae, that he didn't want to hear about it, but he heard him out.

"It's from Chet Donnelly."

He had to call Rae. His original plan had been to wait until she called him, but now he couldn't do that. After talking to Greg, he went back into his living room and called her.

"Good morning," she answered, her voice not betraying if she had seen the video or not.

"Good morning, I need to talk to you about something."

"I know. Melody showed me the video."

He swallowed. He wanted to talk about this. He needed to hear what she thought, but, once again, their timing was off.

"We need to talk about the video, but before that, I need to tell you something. I got a message from Chet."

Thirty minutes later, they were in his Jeep leaving Cool Springs, headed to Fort Worth, Texas to see Chet and try to bring him home with them. The message from him sounded like the ramblings of an unstable person. Gabriel's heart broke as he read it. It was a long, paranoid diatribe that went on and on about how people in the government were spying on him and how his neighbor was planning on poisoning his dog, but then it was interspersed with logical-sounding phrases about fond memories he had of Gabriel and Rae and how much he missed them. It sounded as if their old friend needed help, and Gabriel wanted to do anything he could, and Rae did too.

Besides, Gabriel reasoned as he drove southbound on I-35, he had a three-hour drive to convince her to fall in love with him.

If only he had the guts to bring it up. For the first hour they talked about their old friend Chet. What could have happened to him – could he have fallen into drug use – could he be suffering from a mental condition – could it be some sort of spiritual issue. It was all so bizarre. They would soon see their friend whom they had assumed they would never see again. Why had he left in the first place, and what had he been up to all these years?

Then, for the second hour they talked about Beckham's baseball team, the Cool Springs High School football team's chances of making the playoffs next season, how he needed a haircut, her new favorite coffee order, and a myriad of other topics that were really mere substitutes for what they really wanted to talk about. Finally, with less than an hour left to the drive, she brought it up.

"So, are we ever going to talk about your little video, or are we going to keep pretending it didn't happen?"

He pressed his lips together and snuck a quick look at her. In the seat next to him, she stared him down with folded arms and an arched eyebrow.

"Let's talk about it." And just like that, the pressure that had been built up in every joint of his body released like someone had twisted a valve. He didn't know how she would respond, but finally, finally they would talk about it.

She kept quiet, so he started.

"I'm not sure when it began. I think it started before I even recognized it, because I have a vague memory of wondering when you got so pretty when we were about eleven, but I definitely knew how I felt about you a year ago when you were thinking of going on that month-long missions trip overseas, because I got literally sick to my stomach when I thought about you being gone for a month and realized that must mean I love you. Then, after my dad died, I realized how short life was and that I'd been acting like a kid for so long and that you were the most important person in my life, and I wanted to tell you, but I didn't know how, and I was mad at myself for not doing it sooner, and then you went on a date with that Carter Stayton, and I wanted to hurt him, but I accosted him in a restroom instead like an barbarian, and now I'm just an idiot who is telling you that I love you."

His phone interrupted his speech and told him that their exit was in a mile.

He couldn't look at her. He had vomited his emotions all over her, and didn't want to see the damage. He was certain that she was shell-shocked.

"You know that I love you too," her voice was a whisper, "but I know when it started for me."

She did?

"It was the day you asked me to help you flatten the tires on Brisa's bike."

He laughed. He couldn't help himself.

Her laughter started as giggles and then grew to another one of his favorite laughs of hers, the one where she laughs so hard that tears come out of her eyes and she struggles to catch her breath.

"You were so mad at her. I don't remember what she did, but you snuck a knife out of a drawer in your kitchen and asked me to be the lookout while you stabbed her tires."

"And you were a good lookout," he picked up her hand and squeezed it as they both continued to laugh, "but somehow they figured out that it was us."

"My mom threatened to take away all of my birthday money if I didn't tell her who did it, but I didn't say a word. I kept thinking, *I can't tell on Gabriel, because I love him.*"

Their laughter died down and they grew quiet. His phone told them to exit.

The phone continued to direct them to Chet Donnelly's apartment complex, a series of run-down buildings that looked like somewhere you wouldn't want to be alone at night. Gabriel found the correct building and when he went to park, he noticed that he was still holding her hand. It was silly, but he hated letting go, even for the few seconds it took to pull into the parking space.

They found his apartment, and steadied each other with a shared look. Then, Gabriel knocked. The door opened in a whoosh at the first tap of his knuckles, and their friend's face appeared in the opening.

"Let's go Bulldogs!" Chet Donnelly cheered and jumped out on the landing and hugged both of them at once. "You guys came! How cool is that? That gang is back together! Look at you two. You guys haven't aged a bit."

They couldn't say the same about him. Chet looked a decade older than Gabriel and Rae.

It took Gabriel a second to respond. "We found out last week that you're alive, and now we're here talking to you. I'm not going to lie. It's surreal seeing you, man. It's like seeing a ghost."

"But it's so good to see you," Rae hurriedly added. "If I would've known where you were, I would've reached out a long time ago."

"It's all good. You two will always be my best buds, no matter how much time passes. Am I right?" Before hearing their answer, he pushed the door to his apartment and motioned them inside. "Come on in. Do you guys want a can of Coke?"

The apartment appeared to only have one room. The kitchen, bedroom, and living room were all together in the same room, and it looked like only one person lived there. It was pretty tidy, not how Gabriel imagined it would be when he read Chet's message. He thought they'd be stepping into a ransacked home of a delusional person or a hoarder's nest, but the apartment was surprisingly normal.

They said they would love a Coke, so Chet stepped to the

refrigerator on the kitchen side of the room and grabbed them one. He very sanely handed the cans to them and invited them to have a seat.

As Gabriel sat on the couch next to Rae, he thought that maybe he'd misinterpreted Chet's message or maybe Chet was simply having a bad night when he'd sent the message. Their old friend seemed to be completely fine.

"Your mom said you're expecting a baby?" Rae asked. "That's so exciting. When is she due?"

"She?" Chet asked.

"Your girlfriend? You mom said she was having a baby."

"Oh, yeah, yes." He smiled sheepishly and scratched his head. "Yes, having a baby next month. It's a boy."

"That's awesome, man." Gabriel meant it. "Can you believe you're having a kid?"

Chet laughed. "Not really. It was definitely not planned, but I'm excited. I'm not really set up here to have a kid, so she's going to, you know, be taking care of him at her house, but, yeah, I'm going to go over there a lot and visit. I think she's going to let me do that. We, yeah, aren't exactly together anymore, so it's not a great situation, but I'm going to try to, you know, be a good dad."

Gabriel took a sip of Coke. His old friend's mannerisms worried him. He spoke in a halting way and kept scratching his head. It didn't mean that he needed an emergency intervention, though, Gabriel reasoned, it could simply mean that he was nervous to be speaking to them after so many years.

"We'd love to have you come visit us sometime at Cool Springs," Gabriel told him. "Come back and see how everything has changed. A lot of our old friends are still there, and they'd love to see you."

Chet nodded. "Yeah, I want to. I'd like to catch up with Ty, Chance, and Brooklyn. Are any of them still around?"

"Yes, all but Chance. He stayed in California after college, but the rest are all still there. Brooklyn owns her own bakery and married a guy named Jonah, and they have a new baby." Rae filled him in. "And Ty recently took over his dad's company, and he's married now, too."

"Wow," Chet shook his head. "Everybody's an adult now."

They talked for a while longer, and Gabriel decided that

Chet was fine. The bizarre message from him must have been a false alarm. He didn't regret taking the trip, though. If something had been wrong with Chet, he would have hated himself if he hadn't tried to help him.

Chet asked about their lives, and they told him about their jobs, and then he told them about his efforts to start his own business. He said that he'd had a series of jobs, but never found anything he liked, so he'd decided to start his own business. He explained his vision of an online t-shirt company, which sounded like a perfectly sane, logical business idea.

"You guys want to go out to dinner?" Rae proposed. "We passed a Mexican restaurant on the way here, and I need to satisfy a quesadilla craving."

The guys agreed that they were hungry. The three friends stood to go, and Gabriel opened the apartment door and took a step onto the landing outside.

"What are you doing?" Chet yelled at him and threw his body against the door, slamming it shut. He spun around at them, panting, his face marked with fear. "You can't open the door and walk outside like that! My neighbor is trying to kill me. You always, always check first to make sure it's safe."

He ran to the window next to the door and peeped through the slit between the curtains.

"Thank God. No one's there, so the coast is clear." He turned back to them with total sincerity. "But don't do that again. I told you about my neighbor in my message. I've got to watch every move I make." He pinched the curtains tight and then went to a sensor of some sort that hung high on the wall next to the window. He fiddled with it and then sighed. "I've got the stealth mode set up now, so the apartment is secure. We can go out to eat now, and my team will notify me if my neighbor or the government tries to enter by force."

Rae shot wide eyes to Gabriel, asking the wordless question, *What was wrong with Chet?*

Gabriel had no idea what was wrong with Chet, but he knew this was what they'd traveled all this way for. They had to get him home and in to a doctor or to someone who could help.

Dinner at the Mexican restaurant near Chet's apartment was normal. He didn't act paranoid at all. He didn't verbalize any outlandish fears, but Gabriel could tell from the way his eyes darted wildly about the restaurant that his unfounded fear was still there, bubbling just under the surface.

At dinner, Rae began talking about how it was Mother's Day weekend and that Cool Springs was only a three-hour drive and how much Chet's parents would love to see him. Chet admitted that he didn't have a car, and both Rae and Gabriel assured him that he could ride with them and that figuring out a way back would be simple, and by the end of the meal, they had successfully convinced him to come home with them.

After dinner they returned to the apartment and helped Chet pack a small suitcase. He seemed excited about the trip, but as they were getting into Gabriel's Jeep, he noticed a white SUV with dark tinted windows and had another episode.

"It's them!" He rushed to the side of the Jeep and knelt to the ground. "Get in! Get in!"

They all jumped in the vehicle, and Gabriel drove away as if they were being pursued by corrupt government forces.

"It's probably a good idea that I'm getting out of town," Chet concluded after they'd driven a few miles. "I haven't decided if the surveillance is state or federal, so it's especially good that you're getting me out of the state."

From the back seat, Rae shared a sad smile with Gabriel in the rearview mirror.

"You guys probably don't even know why I left, do you?" He didn't wait for them to respond. "It was, yeah, a combination of a lot of things. I was angry with my parents. I felt rejected by you," he nodded to Rae and continued, "and I was jealous of you," he nodded to Gabriel. "Leaving like that was the dumbest thing I've ever done, and I realized that after a few years, but by then I thought it was too late to go back. After so much time, and after refusing contact with my parents for so long, how could I come crawling back? Yeah, at some point I reasoned that I would only go back home if I could come back as an independent success, but that never materialized. I always loved my parents and my old friends, but the timing never felt right. Now I see that you shouldn't wait for the right time to apologize and tell people you love them."

He rested his forehead on the glass of the passenger side

window and continued quietly, as if talking to himself, "I think when you cut people out of your life it does something to you. Your heart gets hard or something, man. Then you start doing stupid stuff to make your heart feel better, but nothing works, yeah, nothing works."

As Chet talked, Gabriel snuck glances back at Rae. He wished they could talk. Chet was right. You shouldn't wait for the right time to apologize and tell someone you love them. He'd realized the day before that pride was the reason he'd waited so long for the right time. He'd been waiting for a time that he could admit his love for her without having to make himself vulnerable, but with his soul-bearing YouTube video he'd humbled himself and admitted his love for her to the entire world, and she had said that she loved him too, but then . . . He racked his brain analyzing how she had responded. She'd admitted that she had loved him since childhood. They had held hands. But what did that mean? Did she love him like a brother, or did she *love him*, love him?

It drove him crazy that even though they'd said they loved each other, he still didn't know what that meant. He still didn't know what was next for them. Could they actually be more than friends?

He looked at her again in the rearview mirror. She was talking on her phone. The sun was shining through the car window on her, making her light brown hair glisten. She was talking with someone about her work. He caught snippets of her conversation about a Philips project and phishing emails, and then he heard her say the name, "Carter."

"I know you do, Carter, and I agree."

She was talking to Carter Stayton? Or could there be another Carter she worked with?

Next to him, Chet was talking about forgiving his parents and seeing them again, and he knew he should be paying attention to him and encouraging him, but instead he was focused on Rae in the backseat, trying to figure out what she was saying to Carter Stayton.

"Yes, Carter, I'm ready to make a commitment. It's time."

A commitment? To Carter Stayton?

Chapter Nineteen

Rae arrived to church early since she was scheduled to serve as a greeter that morning. As she pulled into the parking lot, she thought about the conversation she'd had with Gabriel the night before. Chet had been listening to their every word from the backseat, so they couldn't say everything on their hearts, but when he pulled his Jeep into her driveway he made a startling admission.

"Before you go, I want to tell you one more thing. Last night I finally realized that my focus has been fixed on the wrong things all these years. I probably won't get everything right immediately, but from now on I'm going to try to get my priorities straight." He picked up her hand and held it as he promised, "I never want to take you for granted again. In fact, I want to be the one who always –

From the backseat, Chet interrupted, "Hey guys, is it just me or is that bush really suspicious looking?"

They said goodnight, and she went inside, and Gabriel took Chet home. He texted her hours later saying that dropping Chet off at his parents' house had taken a while. He and the Donnellys had to convince Chet that the house was safe. He said that he wanted to talk to her more about the video, but that he understood she needed time to process everything.

When she entered the church lobby, she saw that Family Chapel went all out for Mother's Day. Every year they did something special, but this year they went above and beyond. They usually had a photo booth and a flower for every woman, but this year they had an antique truck set up in the lobby as a do-it-yourself flower bouquet bar. All women were invited to create their own bouquets from the colorful fresh-cut flowers that were billowing out of the back of the bright turquoise truck.

Rae appreciated how the church always made sure to honor all women and not just mothers every year on Mother's Day. Their pastors, Kevin and Maureen, didn't have children themselves, and so they seemed to intentionally ensure that no one felt left out or isolated on a holiday that could be painful for some.

She clipped on her Family Chapel volunteer nametag in the church coffee shop while her mom's old friend, Pam Miller, made her a cup of coffee.

"Did you hear the news?" Pam asked while she frothed Rae's latte. "Cameron and Hannah are expecting! I'm going to be a grandma in July!"

She squealed as she handed Rae her coffee, and Rae congratulated her and then chuckled to herself as she thought about Pam Miller making her announcement to everyone who would get a coffee that morning. She didn't know if that was the way Hannah and Cameron intended to tell the world, but who told future grandmas what to do?

She found her assigned post at the double door entrance on the west side of the main lobby and armed herself with a stack of the welcome brochures for visitors and Pastor Kevin's sermon notes for anyone who wanted them. She also re-filled the supply of paper bags that hung next to the entrance for people to take home and fill up with groceries and bring back for the food pantry for the needy.

As Rae opened the door for the early arrivers and shook hands and said, "Good morning," she couldn't stop herself from constantly scanning the parking lot for the Jeep with Gabriel's face on it. She felt like she was in limbo with him. They'd confessed their feelings, or had they? They both said that they loved each other, but was it a romantic love or a best friend, next door neighbor love? She was at the point now where she didn't know if it even mattered. She was moving. In a month she would be living in another state, and Gabriel would still be here with his admirers, and maybe that was the way it was supposed to be all along. Maybe love didn't always result in a life of happily ever after together.

As Rae watched the entrance, a small gray sedan with an Uber placard in the window pulled in under the main entrance awning and her younger sister, Claire, stepped out of the car.

"Claire!" Rae rushed outside to greet her sister whom she hadn't seen in person since Christmas.

"My Ray of Sunshine!" Claire yelled her cheesy nickname for her sister as Rae threw her arms around her. "Might not want to hug me too tightly. I am stinky from the airplane."

"Oh whatever, I haven't seen you in five months. I don't care how stinky you are."

They laughed as they hugged, and Rae felt a little catch in her throat and water in her eyes. She didn't realize until that moment how much she'd missed Claire. Sure, they'd talked on the phone, but it was different than actually seeing her in person and getting to hug her.

"Are you greeting today?" Claire asked, pointing to Rae's name badge.

"Yes, Maureen roped me into serving on the team. You know how impossible it is to say no to her."

"Oh yes. Remember the year she convinced me to be on the puppet team at Vacation Bible School? My arm still hurts from that, and I'm sure a whole generation of Family Chapel kids are traumatized by that creepy-looking Miss Mary Martha puppet and her giant google eyes and purple yarn hair."

They laughed again at the memory, and Claire told her that she was going to go sit in their mom's usual spot to surprise her. Lois was expecting her youngest child to arrive after church, and she was going to be so happy when she saw that Claire had arrived early to be in service with her. The sisters slung arms over each other's shoulders and Claire dragged her little suitcase behind them as they walked inside.

"Where's your sidekick?" Claire asked, looking around the lobby.

"My sidekick?" Rae didn't know who she meant. She couldn't remember anyone ever being called that.

Claire put a hand on her hip and smirked at her sister. "Oh come on. You know who I mean. Gabriel, your sidekick. If you're here, then he's got to be around here somewhere."

"Gabriel, my sidekick?" Rae shook her head. "I think you mean the other way around. Didn't you say something recently about me holding out hope for him?"

Claire grasped both of her sister's shoulders and lightly shook her. "Ugh, will you stop with that! That's not what I meant. I meant that I've been holding out hope that both of you would open your eyes and get over the past. When will you ever see that he's the one who's been following you around all these years?

You're the one who is perfectly content and self-assured. He's the one who needs your constant attention and approval. Seriously, sis, forget about high school. Those days are over, and if you reciprocated that guy's affection in the slightest, then he would turn his life upside down to be with you."

Claire pecked her on the cheek and went into the auditorium to wait on their mother, and Rae returned to her assigned post and put on a welcoming smile. Her thoughts were on what Claire had said, though. Was her sister right? Had everything really changed since they were kids, and was she the only one who hadn't realized it?

"Hello! Earth to Rae!"

A hand waved in front of her face bringing her back to the good ol' Family Chapel lobby.

The pastor's wife, Maureen, stood in front of her with a giant lipsticked smile, pearl necklace, and pink sweater set.

"I think your body is here, but your mind is somewhere else, girly. Is everything okay, honey?"

Rae gave her an embarrassed laugh. "Yes ma'am. My mind was definitely somewhere else. How are you this morning, Maureen?"

"I've already had two cups of coffee, and I'm headed to get a third from Pam." She nodded toward the coffee bar where Pam Miller was proclaiming her baby news to a group of church-goers. "It's going to be a wonderful day. Do you have special plans with your mom today?"

Rae thought about the lunch and the bargain. An image of herself seated next to Dustin Henderson at the table across from Gabriel and a strange woman came to mind, and she felt sick to her stomach.

"We're having lunch together this afternoon, with the Matthews."

"Of course you are," Maureen said with a knowing look. "You and that cutie-pie, Gabriel, are quite the pair, aren't you? Why don't you two quit the funny stuff and just go for it?"

Rae choked at her words and coughed. "Excuse me? Funny stuff?"

Maureen swatted at Rae's arm. "Oh my stars, you know what I mean. Everyone knows how you two feel about each other.

It's been written all over your faces for years. Just go ahead and date the boy, Rae."

The middle-aged pastor's wife wrinkled her nose at Rae and then swished her hips as she sashayed away, leaving Rae speechless.

Rae stood staring after Maureen for a few seconds, still smelling her Estee Lauder scent, until someone entered the church and she had to get back to her job, but she couldn't stop thinking about Maureen's words.

Quit the funny stuff and just go for it.

Maureen didn't know that it wasn't that simple.

Through the glass doors she saw what she knew she would eventually see that morning – Gabriel's Jeep entering the parking lot. The sticker-covered vehicle parked, and Gabriel got out and walked toward the building. She read his posture and manner as he walked. Hands stuffed deep into pockets and chin tucked low into his chest, it looked like he was glum about something.

She opened the door and greeted him. "Good morning and welcome to Family Chapel. Happy Mother's Day."

"Hey," he mumbled and kept his hands in his pockets.

"How is Chet?" Maybe Chet's condition had him down. It certainly was sobering seeing their old friend like that.

"I haven't heard from him this morning, but last night when I took him to his parent's house, Joe promised that they'd all be here at church today."

"That's good."

He gave her elbow a squeeze and went toward the coffee bar. She continued faithfully serving as people streamed into the church. The crowd was larger than normal with several kids and grandkids visiting church with their moms and grandmas, and lots of people wore pastel colored clothes in honor of the day. Between the ladies carrying around the bouquets from the flower bar, the cheerful-colored clothes, and the joyful family members chatting in the lobby, it seemed as if everyone in the world was happy this morning.

Then Rae caught sight of the one person who seemed to be unhappy. Gabriel. He was standing on the opposite end of the lobby sipping his coffee like a dark cloud in an otherwise clear sky.

What was his problem?

Sounds of music flooded the lobby and the crowd began making their way to the sanctuary. The service was beginning.

Rae wrapped up her duties, shaking the hands of the final latecomers and tidying the lobby area, and then she started toward the back doors of the auditorium to her usual seat next to her mother.

Gabriel stopped her.

"I know this isn't the time, but," he paused and then continued, "no, I'm sorry. We'll talk about it later. This isn't the right time."

"Let's talk now. I'll be worried about it all morning if we don't just go ahead and deal with it."

He hesitated, looking around the church lobby that was nearly empty now. His eyes looked tired, like he'd been unable to sleep much the night before.

She put a hand on his arm. "Are you okay?" It hurt to see him so upset.

"Yesterday you said something on the phone to Carter Stayton that's been bothering me. You told him that you were ready to commit? That it was time to make a commitment?"

He looked absolutely miserable. She should have felt a bit happy about his misery, since she'd been miserable over him many times, but she couldn't gloat when the love of her life was hurting. She had planned on telling him about the job in Georgia, but the time hadn't been right yet. Timing had always been their problem.

"I wanted to talk to you about this. I didn't want to tell you in the middle of the church lobby, but I've accepted a job in Savannah. I'm going to be their IT Director."

His face fell, but then he gathered himself and put on a proud smile.

"IT Director at thirty-four, huh? That's young for that position, right? But I've always said you were the smart one. Congrats, Spence."

He kissed her cheek when he congratulated her, and a rush of warmth filled her. She loved his nearness, but knew not to mistake it for a promise. This was a goodbye kiss.

He pulled away, but she touched his arm to stop him.

"Wait, Gabriel, I need to tell you – "

"You two playing hooky out here?" Charlie's voice

interrupted her. He held sleeping baby Caroline in his arms and wore a what-are-you-guys-up-to smirk.

"We were just going inside," Gabriel answered before she could say anything and pushed the sanctuary door open and held it so she could enter before him.

She wanted to finish her statement. She wanted to tell him that she'd taken the job because she knew that even though they loved each other that they probably needed to give up on any kind of romance between them. It wasn't supposed to be this hard. People who fell in love and lived happily ever after surely didn't have all of these issues with timing and misunderstandings, but, like always, it wasn't the time to say any of that. Church service was in full swing, and he was holding the door open for her, so she entered without a word.

Family Chapel had a rotating line-up of volunteers who led the music portion of their services, and today's leader was Jonah Walters who was married to Rae's old friend, Brooklyn. In Rae's opinion he was one of the best, and she wished he could be the permanent worship leader, but he was also a firefighter with Charlie, so he had to miss when he was at the fire station. He was leading a slow song about welcoming God into their hearts as Rae and Gabriel walked to the row occupied by their families.

She stepped into the row next to her mom who sent her a question with a raised eyebrow, silently asking what had taken her so long. Rae slightly inclined her head behind her toward Gabriel who had followed her in, and her mom closed her eyes and shook her head, as if annoyed at Rae and Gabriel's constant back and forth.

Rae was annoyed by it too, but as she began to sing along with the congregation, her annoyance washed away. She truly meant the words of the song which called out to God to enter her heart, and felt her attitude change as she sang. She didn't know how everything was going to work out, but a peace overtook her heart, and she knew that God would somehow work everything out for good.

The music ended and the congregation sat. The row was so full that Gabriel's body was right next to hers without any space between them. It should have felt uncomfortable, but instead it felt right.

"Sorry, it's so crowded," he whispered while the pastor started talking, "would you like me to sit somewhere else?"

She couldn't imagine him sitting anywhere other than right beside her.

She shook her head and gave him a small smile. "No, it's fine."

She tried to focus her attention on Pastor Kevin, but it was difficult with Gabriel so close.

"On Mother's Day I usually share a message centered on moms and their unique role in our lives, so we often study Proverbs thirty-one on this day, or we learn from bible characters like Hannah or Mary, but today I feel compelled to go a different direction. Today, we are once again going to read and study from a book I just can't seem to get away from lately, the book of First Corinthians. We will be looking at chapter thirteen this morning."

Rae turned in her bible to the familiar passage and chuckled at their pastor. He'd been so enamored with the two letters to the Corinthians lately that they should have all seen this coming.

"Let's all stand for the reading of the word." Pastor Kevin instructed, and the congregation stood, most of them holding open bibles in their hands.

The pastor began reading the familiar chapter about love, describing the preeminence and endurance of love. He read the entire chapter which ended with verse thirteen which declared that at the end faith, hope, and love will remain, and that love was the greatest of all, even over the extremely important qualities of faith and hope.

The pastor prayed, and the congregation sat, and he began his message.

"A lot of times, life is hard. We might lose a job or get a divorce or our parent might die."

Rae gave Gabriel's knee a little pat.

"We might have financial trouble. We might get into a disagreement with someone we really love that causes a rift in the relationship which makes us drift apart."

At that moment, Rae noticed Joe, Paige, and Chet Donnelly sitting side-by-side in a pew two rows ahead of them.

"Sometimes the small, silly stuff can get between us, like your relative who you really love can get under your skin with their little idiosyncrasies." Pastor Kevin winked and jerked his head toward the first row where his wife Maureen sat, and she pretended to be offended, and the congregation laughed.

Rae looked down the row at Brisa and chuckled.

Pastor Kevin continued, "Sometimes the roles we've always played in relationships shift and we have to figure out how to stay close to each other and continue to respect one another, despite the changing nature of our relationship."

Rae leaned forward and glanced down at Claire who shared a smile with her and winked.

"Sometimes our relationships are hindered by miscommunication or bad timing."

Rae's back stiffened, and she didn't dare a glance to her left in Gabriel's direction.

"But, according to this chapter," Pastor Kevin continued, "nothing can stop love. On this Mother's Day, I want families and friends and husbands and wives to remember that love is the key ingredient. The bible tells us that God is love, and that if we say we love God who we can't see, then we must absolutely love our neighbors who we do see."

Rae looked around the room at her neighbors who were all intently listening to the message. Jonah and Brooklyn and Cameron and Hannah and their families, the Martinez family, the Donnellys, the Matthews, her mother, and dozens of others who she loved. She hoped she expressed love to them all like the pastor was challenging them to do.

"And not only does Jesus tell us to love our family and friends, he tells us that even sinners can do that, but he challenges us to love our enemies, those who disagree with us and make our lives difficult." The pastor intertwined his hands and continued softly, "Isn't that what Jesus did? And aren't we called to be like him?"

The sermon continued, but Rae's mind drifted. A four-word phrase Pastor Kevin said earlier echoed in her mind: *Nothing can stop love*. She wrote the phrase in the margin of her bible next to verse eight, which read, "Love never fails."

As she wrote and then underlined the phrase, she pondered the concept. Was love enough? Could it really overcome misunderstandings and bad timing and even . . .distance? She looked at the Donnellys again and marveled at the way God had restored their relationships. Her mother had told her that Paige told her she and Joe were going to do everything they could to help Chet. He was probably moving back in with them, and already had an appointment to speak with Pastor Kevin and see what kind of recovery programs they could help him with. It would likely be a difficult road to healing for Chet, but Rae knew that God could heal him, and that Chet would get his redemption story. His parents and the people in this church loved him too much to let him fall away again. Pastor Kevin was right. Nothing can stop love.

He concluded the sermon with a call to repentance, for them all to repent of times they hadn't shown love and to ask the Holy Spirit to empower them to love the way Jesus did. The majority of the congregation took time to pray quietly in their seats or at the front of the auditorium. Rae and Gabriel both prayed in their pew. She bowed her head and prayed, and next to her Gabriel leaned forward with elbows on his knees and prayed as well.

She wondered if his prayers matched hers? She prayed for God to give her direction concerning her job and spent most of her prayer time asking God to someway, somehow make a way for her and Gabriel to be together.

After she finished praying, her mother whispered to her, "Could you drive me home? I rode with Evelyn, but she wants to stop by Fresh Market on the way home, and I need to take the ham out of the oven." She tapped the plain wristwatch she wore. "Pastor went a little long today, and I've got a spiral cut honey glazed ham that's going to be all dried out if I don't get home soon."

Rae nodded that she could ride with her, and they stood and exited reverently, not wanting to interrupt anyone still praying. In the lobby, Rae took her mom's arm and squeezed it.

"Happy Mother's Day, by the way, to the best mom in the world."

Her mom waved a hand at her to dismiss the compliment, but Rae noticed the upturn of her lips and color in her cheeks.

"You had to be both mom and dad for many years," she told her mom as they left the building and headed toward her car, "and you did it with strength and love and grace. I am very thankful for you, mom. I know that I owe everything I am to you."

"Well, dear, you were a handful, but I survived."

Rae feigned offense with an open mouth, giving her mom the reaction she wanted, and Lois cackled.

They arrived at Rae's car, and Lois stopped her daughter with a pointed finger.

"I'll get in the car and wait for you, dear, but please don't take too long. Remember my ham."

Rae wrinkled her dark eyebrows at her mother. "What do you mean?"

Lois nodded to something behind Rae, and Rae turned to see Gabriel following them at a distance.

"Like I said, tik tock. No one likes dry ham." Lois punctuated her direction with a light tap on her daughter's hand and then got into the front seat of the car.

"Hey Rae, do you have a minute?" Gabriel's voice came from behind.

She turned to him, and even though his was one of the most familiar faces to her, she still felt a slight movement in her heart when she saw him. Would that ever go away? She hoped it wouldn't.

"Well, my mom has informed me that I don't have much more than that. Apparently, she's making a ham for lunch, and it's in danger of drying out." She made a face, and he laughed.

"I just wanted to apologize for my moodiness earlier and to tell you how proud I am of you for your new job. I can't imagine Cool Springs without Rae Spencer, but hopefully we'll find a way to go on."

His words said one thing, but his face didn't match. He looked as if he didn't know how he would go on without her. Part of her wanted to call the whole move off. Tell the Georgia branch that she'd changed her mind. But, as hard as it was to see Gabriel hurting, she knew she was doing the right thing in taking the job. She couldn't continue with things as they'd always been.

"Gabriel, I think Pastor Kevin's message was for us. Nothing can stop love. I may be moving to Savannah, but I still love you, and I believe that somehow our love is going to overcome the distance."

All around them, the parking lot was filled with church goers leaving the building and finding their vehicles. Most were happy and chatting, and some shot looks over to Gabriel and Rae, but no one said anything. Normally, people would call out 'See you next week' or 'Good to see you today,' but no one interrupted them. Rae felt as if everyone could tell something significant was happening with Family Chapel's infamous will-they-or-won't-they couple.

Gabriel put both of his hands on her shoulders, slid them to her elbows, and turned her to face him instead of their church friends. He closed the short distance between them with a step and bent his face to hers, his lips nearly touching her own.

"May I kiss you?"

The warmth of his lips so close to hers sent a tingling sensation through her, and she couldn't speak. So she nodded.

His mouth melted onto hers so sweetly that when he started to pull away, she grabbed his arms and pulled him back. He kissed her; she kissed him back, and then it wasn't clear who was kissing whom, but now that she had finally shared a kiss with Gabriel, she knew she could never, ever, ever go back to not kissing him again.

Chapter Twenty

Gabriel pulled his Jeep into his mother's driveway and parked behind Brisa's minivan. Before killing the engine, he looked next door and saw Rae's little white car in her mother's driveway and sighed.

He got out of the vehicle and hit the button on his key fob to lock it, and stopped. His black Jeep, which he had loved for years was now a monstrosity. He hated the stupid sticker that wrapped the entire vehicle. Three images of his own giant smiling face covered both sides and the back, and suddenly, he wanted them gone.

He found a corner of the sticker at the bottom of the driver's side door and started to pull. The enormous sticker sheet lifted in one piece. He yanked at it and the entire driver's side sticker was now gone, revealing the shiny black car that was underneath. He wrapped the sticker into a big ball and then went to work on the back and then the passenger side.

Finished, he stepped back and inspected his clean Jeep. Brisa's Sticker Cutie product had indeed peeled off in one piece without leaving behind a trace, as advertised. He punched the three sticker sheets into one big ball and felt a sense of relief. It would be nice to be able to drive around without constantly sporting pictures of himself like a decorated convertible in a homecoming parade.

As he walked to the front porch and neared the door of his mom's house, he heard his family before he saw any of them. He chuckled to himself. No one had ever accused any of the Matthews of being timid or soft spoken. He stepped inside his childhood home and the memories echoed back to him from everywhere – the recliner where his dad had sat every evening and watched the ten o'clock news and the wall of framed pictures of family vacations and baby pictures and graduation photos all reminders that this place that might not look too special to anybody else was very special to him.

"Uncle Gabriel!" Beckham ran from the kitchen through the

living room to him. "Come in here. Grandma just said that she made a bargain with you to bring a date and that after she's done fixing you up with a woman, she's fixing me up with a woman!" The eleven-year-old's eyes were wide in fear. "I don't want to be fixed up with a woman!"

He tousled the kid's light brown hair and laughed. "You tell Grandma that you don't need her to fix you up with a woman, because you're going to leave that up to God. If He wants you to have a wife one day, then He will bring her to you."

"Oh, Uncle Gabriel, that's a good one. I'm going to tell her that!" He ran away at the same speed he stole bases, and once again Gabriel laughed at his nutty family.

In the familiar kitchen all of the people he loved sat crammed around a too-small table. Lois's perfectly moist ham was the star in the center of his family's old wooden table, and it was surrounded by a dozen side dishes that he was certain his sisters and mother had provided. The matching dining chairs held the adults, and the three kids sat in patio chairs that someone had drug in from outside.

All of the seats were filled except one, which was next to Rae, so he slid into it, the memory of their first and only kiss overtaking his thoughts.

"Now that my baby brother is here," Brisa announced as she stood from her seat.

"Oh no. Not another sales pitch," he whispered to Rae.

She responded with an elbow in his ribs.

Brisa shot him a withering look and continued, "Let's give our moms their gifts." She picked up a shiny purple bag and handed it to their mom. "Here you go, mom. This is from all of us, even the kids helped pick it out."

"Thank you, dear." Evelyn took the gift from her eldest daughter and winked at Beckham. "So, you picked this out for grandma, huh?"

He nodded, but one of his twin sisters objected.

"No, he didn't! Only mama got the present, and me and Bella picked out the bag. Beckham and daddy didn't even come to the store with us."

"Hush, Brinley," Brisa shushed her daughter.

Gabriel heard Rae stifle a giggle that turned into a little snort.

Evelyn pulled a set of placemats and a stack of coordinating dish towels out of the bag. She complimented the color and quality and thanked Brisa and her family, and she immediately hung one of the dish towels on the handle of the oven door to show them how much she loved it.

Next up, Charlie handed her a gift in a Fresh Market sack, apologizing for not wrapping it.

Camila, who sat next to him holding their sleeping baby, added, "It's not much, mom. Sorry about that. We will do better for your birthday."

"Oh poo," Evelyn waved a hand at her. "Don't say that. This is your first Mother's Day. We should all be honoring you today."

Evelyn continued opening the gift, and Gabriel thought he saw a tear form in his sister's eye.

His mom pulled a vase of bright flowers out of the bag and gasped.

"Oh my! These are gorgeous." She stepped over to the island in the middle of the kitchen and sat the flowers on the center of it. "They liven up the whole room. Thank you so much, dears. Now, who's ready to eat this delicious ham that Lois made?"

The men and kids cheered, but Brisa and Camila objected.

"Hold on a minute." Camila stopped them.

"Yeah, wait a second. What about Gabriel and Rae's gifts?" Brisa wanted to know. "They clearly didn't hold up their end of the bargain you made with them. So, they should have brought gifts."

Sometimes Gabriel wished Brisa was a brother so he could smack her.

Rae held up both hands like she was surrendering. "I told my mom that I didn't have a date. The agreement was that she would provide a date for me if I couldn't find one. I can't help it if she couldn't scrounge up a date for me."

"Same goes for me," Gabriel added. "I tried online dating; I almost brought a woman I met at the grocery store – "

"Whose name he couldn't remember," Rae informed them.

"I called her the Bread Woman."

Everyone laughed, and Evelyn held out a hand to settle them.

"You two don't seem to understand." She gave her best friend a conspiratorial smile. "Our plan worked perfectly. After a week of searching, you two are sitting next to each other. Doesn't that tell you something?"

Lois chimed in. "Exactly. We wanted you two to see what everyone else sees. You're perfect for each other."

"Lois and I knew that you two would be sitting next to each other at this luncheon, and we," she paused and threw an arm around her best friend's shoulder, "We, your mothers, wanted to show you what you've been overlooking all along."

Gabriel looked around the table. His two sisters, two brothers-in-law, nephew, two nieces, and even baby Caroline all seemed to agree that he and Rae belonged together.

But, most importantly, he knew they belonged together, and he wanted to be wherever she was, even if that meant leaving Cool Springs.

He stood.

"Well, maybe this isn't the best time for this, since it's Mother's Day we should probably be focused on all of the moms around the table, but I've made a decision." He looked down at Rae who was looking up at him with those intense dark eyes of hers. Her beautiful red lips were pressed together in a line, as if she had no idea what he was about to say. "I'm moving to Georgia."

Her beautiful red lips fell open.

"Savannah, to be exact."

Evelyn narrowed her eyes at him in confusion, but Lois's mouth fell open like her daughter's, and then she covered it with her hand. Then, Lois put a hand on her best friend's arm.

"Evelyn, dear, I know what's happening. Rae got a job in Georgia, and," she paused and looked at Gabriel. "He's going with her."

Nearly every family member gasped, except Charlie who said that he knew it, and Evelyn who crossed her arms and nodded in approval, as if she had set the whole thing up herself.

Brisa wasn't so sure. "But what about your business? And your family? Everyone you know lives here. You've never lived anywhere else."

He sat in his seat next to Rae and addressed her only.

"That is, I want to move to Savannah, if that's what you want. The problem is, Rae Spencer, that I can't imagine living away from you. I can find a job or build a business anywhere. I love my family, and I'll miss them a lot, but if I didn't have you in my life I don't know how I could function." He picked up her hand and held it in his. "So, do you mind if I tag along to Georgia with you?"

"Now, hold on a second," his mom interjected.

Gabriel answered his mom's objection before she verbalized it. "Separately, of course. My mother raised a gentleman. I'm not suggesting we shack up."

Then Rae laughed his favorite laugh of hers – the one where a soft giggle bubbled up out of her and her cheeks turned pink, and he knew he wanted to continue cataloguing her laughs, her tears, her jokes, her facial expressions, her sarcastic comments, and everything else about Rae Spencer for the rest of his life.

*****

Rae couldn't help it. She had to laugh. When Gabriel asked if he could move to Georgia with her and then assured his mom he wasn't 'shaking up,' she cracked up.

The thought of Gabriel Matthews, the guy she had followed around like a lovesick puppy dog for her entire life now following her? Well, she had to laugh.

She told herself not to rush this moment. She wanted to remember every detail – his denim-colored eyes so serious, the way his hand felt holding hers, the nearness of him new yet familiar around the table where they'd done homework together as kids, surrounded by their shocked families – she took time to breathe it in before she answered him.

"I would love to have you come to Georgia with me, because I don't want life without you in it. There's no one I'd rather run out of gas with or play pickleball with or go to church with or go grocery shopping with. I want us to figure out a new city together, and I want to dream about the future together, because the fact is, that I love you, Gabriel, and I always have."

For their first kiss he had asked permission, but she didn't bother with that now. For all of her earlier thoughts about savoring the moment, she couldn't wait to kiss him again. She half-stood out of her chair and kissed him, not thinking about anything besides the fact that the pastor had been right. Nothing could stop love.

Gabriel wrapped his arms around her, pulling her into his lap, and around the table the family cheered.

"I told you all this was going to happen!" Beckham announced.

"I'd say our bargain was a success, Lois, don't you think?" Evelyn asked her friend.

"An absolute success," Lois agreed with her friend, and then the two of them clinked their tea cups together and cackled.

Epilogue
One Year Later

"Mom!" Beckham ran into his grandma's kitchen where his mom sat at the table talking to grandma, Aunt Camila, and Ms. Lois. "Have you seen my glove? We have to leave for my game in fifteen minutes, and I can't find my glove anywhere." His voice held a panicky tone, betraying the fear he felt at starting in his very first middle school baseball game. It felt so much more important than Little League, and he was terrified he would mess everything up, especially since his whole family was going to be there watching.

"It's in your bag. I saw you pack it this morning." His mom smiled at him. "Calm down, honey. Everything is going to be fine."

He took a deep breath and tried to steady himself, listening to the women in the kitchen as he tried to achieve calm.

"They should be here any minute," Grandma informed the ladies as she checked the time on the microwave. "Gabriel told me they wanted to meet us all here before we left for the game."

"I'm glad they were able to come a couple of days early." Rae's sister, Claire said, because Uncle Gabriel and Rae were coming on Friday before Mother's Day even though they weren't supposed to be there until Sunday. "They've been so busy. I haven't seen them since Christmas, but I've talked to them both on the phone a lot. It sounds like Rae is doing great at her new job, and Gabriel's business is booming. I'm so happy for them."

"I know. I'm happy for them too." Aunt Camila agreed. "And dad would be so proud of Gabriel for starting his own brokerage."

His mom smiled at her sister. "Matthews Realty. Can you imagine how proud dad would be?"

"Gabriel was insistent that we all be here. Do you girls

know if your husbands will be here?" Grandma asked her daughters who definitely weren't girls.

Beckham's mom and Aunt Camila reminded grandma that his dad and Uncle Charlie were in the backyard talking to the men who were installing the new in-ground pool, and Beckham didn't understand how grandma couldn't remember that. They'd all been talking about the men outside overseeing the pool construction. It seemed like grandma was forgetting a lot lately.

"Oh that's right." Grandma clicked her tongue. "Brisa, I don't know why you had to spend so much of your Sticker Cutie money on that fancy pool. The grandkids like the water hose and the sprinklers I got from Fresh Market just fine."

His mom sighed, and Beckham knew what that sigh meant. He had heard his mom make that same sigh when she was irritated with something his dad had said but she was asking Jesus to help her be nice.

"Mom, everyone will enjoy this pool for years to come. Besides," his mom paused and wiggled her shoulders like she did when she was about to brag on one of his homeruns, "Like I always tell my thousands of Cutie Partners, you can't take it with you. If your bills are paid, and you have a solid savings plan and a steady income stream, then you should spend that money and enjoy life to the fullest."

His mom's voice rose and fell like it did when she was talking to all of her Sticker Cutie partners. It seemed everyone couldn't believe the money his mom was making on selling stickers, but he wasn't going to say anything bad about stickers, because like his mom said, their family was laughing all the way to the Sticker Cutie bank.

His twin sisters ran into the kitchen and hollered at the tops of their lungs that Uncle Gabriel was here. Bella and Brinley had really missed Uncle Gabriel, and they'd been camped out on Grandma's driveway all day watching for his Jeep to come driving down Redbud Circle.

Beckham half-ran to the front door. He wanted to all-out run, because he also missed Uncle Gabriel and Rae, but he didn't want anyone thinking he was as excited as his sisters. He wasn't a little kid anymore.

Word spread through the house and to the backyard that

Gabriel and Rae had arrived, and in minutes the entire family had gathered on the driveway and cheered when the black Jeep pulled in.

"Hey everyone!" Uncle Gabriel said when he stepped out. "Give me a hug, mom." He hugged grandma and then the rest of them, and then he kissed baby Caroline who was being held by Uncle Charlie and commented that she really wasn't a baby anymore. Beckham hadn't realized it, but Uncle Gabriel was right. His little cousin had pigtails and wore sneakers because she was already walking, actually running, all over the place, and he knew Uncle Charlie was holding her because she was kind of wild and known for running off and hiding.

Rae got out of the car too, and hugged Ms. Lois and Claire. Rae's hair was longer than he'd remembered, and she looked really pretty.

Uncle Gabriel said something about all of them going inside, because he knew they needed to leave soon to get to Beckham's baseball game, and he had something he wanted to tell everyone. Uncle Charlie whistled, for some reason, and Grandma looked like she was about to cry.

Just then, Beckham noticed something.

"Hang on, everybody." He tried to get everyone's attention, but they were ignoring him. Something serious was happening, and he had to tell everyone. This time he yelled as loud as he could, "Everybody! Stop! I need to tell you all something!"

The entire Matthews family and Ms. Lois and her daughters all stopped and turned to look at twelve-year-old Beckham. He swallowed and told them what he had seen.

"Everybody, look at Rae's hand! She's got a big ol' diamond ring on her left hand – her marrying finger!"

Rae held up her left hand and wiggled her fingers, the sun sending sparkles all around.

"You figured it out, Becks," Uncle Gabriel laughed.

Everyone standing on the driveway, now not two families but one, all joined in on the laughter, and Uncle Gabriel scooped Rae up and gave her a big kiss right in the middle of them all.

From the Author

Dear Reader,

  I hope you loved The Mother's Day Bargain. If you haven't read The Mother's Day Letter or The Mother's Day Tea, I think you will really love them if you enjoyed this book. My Mother's Day books are all set in Cool Springs and have some overlapping characters. My next book will tell Claire Spencer's story. I am currently writing it, and it is so much fun writing a book set in London. Stay tuned to my social media to find out when that book will be coming out!

  I want you to know that I am so grateful for you. You are who I spend so much time writing for. As you read my books I pray that you are encouraged and entertained. I am so thankful for everyone who reads my books, everyone who buys my books (even if they are buying them for someone else!), everyone who takes the time to write a review, or recommends my books to a friend, and for everyone who connects with me through social media. The older and more experienced I get, the more grateful I am for all of these people who do so many "little things" to help my writing and publishing journey.

  I am also thankful for my family, which now includes three daughters-in-law! My family continues to be my number one supporters, and I am just so grateful to all of them, especially the world's best husband. I have also been blessed with wonderful friends who often serve as beta readers and listen to my outlandish book ideas with nothing but encouragement. Recently I have found an incredible audiobook narrator, Lisa Lynn Sandlin, who has been fantastic to work with. I am so thankful to her for taking chances on indie authors and for narrating my books so perfectly. I am also thankful to the people of Discovery Church in Yukon, Oklahoma for being my second family. I love doing life with you.

  If you'd like to connect, I'm on Facebook, Instagram, and

Pinterest as Martha Fouts Books. I would love to interact with you there. Also, leaving a review is always a bolster to us indie authors, so if you'd like to post a review to Amazon or Goodreads or some other book site, that would be wonderful.

Writing is a work of the heart for me. It's more than a hobby or a job, and I would still do it if I only had one reader, because, ultimately, everything we do should be for an audience of One. Everything I do, I do it for the Lord.

Happy Reading,

Martha

Made in the USA
Monee, IL
31 March 2025